Mel Bay's

BUILDING RIGHT HAND TECHNIQUE

by Bill Bay

AUTHOR'S NOTE—
BUILDING RIGHT HAND TECHNIQUE

Building Right Hand Technique is a master technical study book for the use of a flat pick. The studies are designed to build *CLEANNESS* and *CLARITY* of sound. Many of the studies are designed to develop ease and agility in playing rapid passages which contain skips from string to string. Other studies are designed to develop right hand picking speed on linear passages. The material contained in this text consists of original studies, works of the great classical guitar masters arranged for plectrum guitar, fiddle tunes, jazz etudes and many other studies in varied styles. Upon completion of this text, the guitarist should have attained flexibility, confidence and accuracy in the right hand. In addition, the general tone quality produced by the pick should have improved to the point where the sound is clear and pronounced and where the player can, with sensitivity and flexibility, alter the tone while picking to the various shades of color desired. The companion text to this book is entitled Building Left Hand Technique. That book also will involve itself with coordination between the left and right hand and it will center more on the linear aspect of guitar technique. I highly recommend studying that text upon completion of this book.

Bill Bay

CONTENTS

PICKING STUDIES

[Play All Studies With ⊓ V ⊓ V Alternate Picking]
Fingerstyle = i-m-i-m or m-a-m-a

Continue This Exercise on All Remaining Strings.

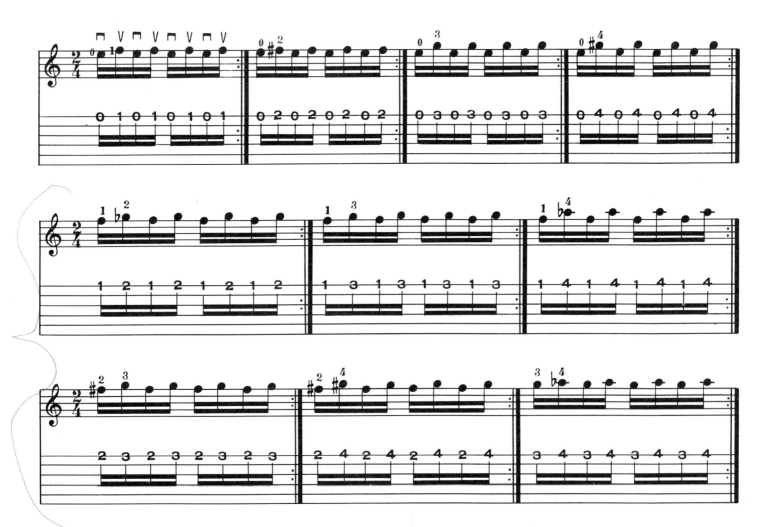

Continue These Exercises on All Remaining Strings.

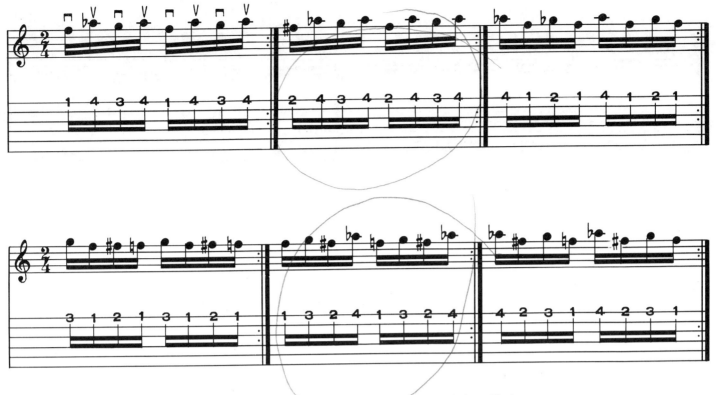

Continue These Exercises on All Remaining Strings.

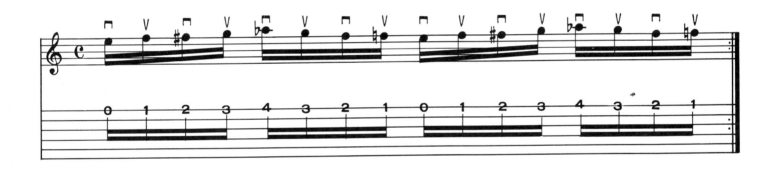

Continue These Exercises on All Remaining Strings.

5

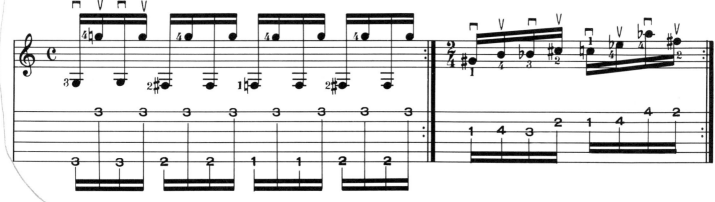

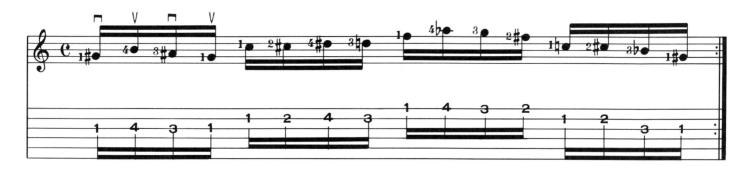

Continue The Above Exercises on All Remaining Strings.

TREMOLO STUDIES

Tremolo studies help build pick control. Try to make each note sound smooth and equal in value. Do not let your hand get overly tense and tight. Imagine that the down up motion is originating from the elbow.

EXAMPLE

TREMOLO STUDY #1

Continue on all remaining strings

TREMOLO STUDY #2

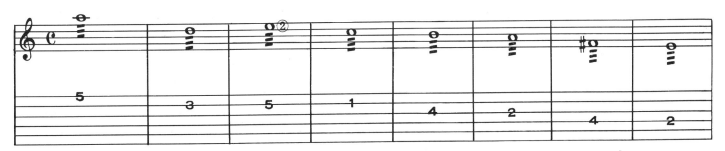

TREMOLO STUDY #3

(Open strings)

A SICILIA

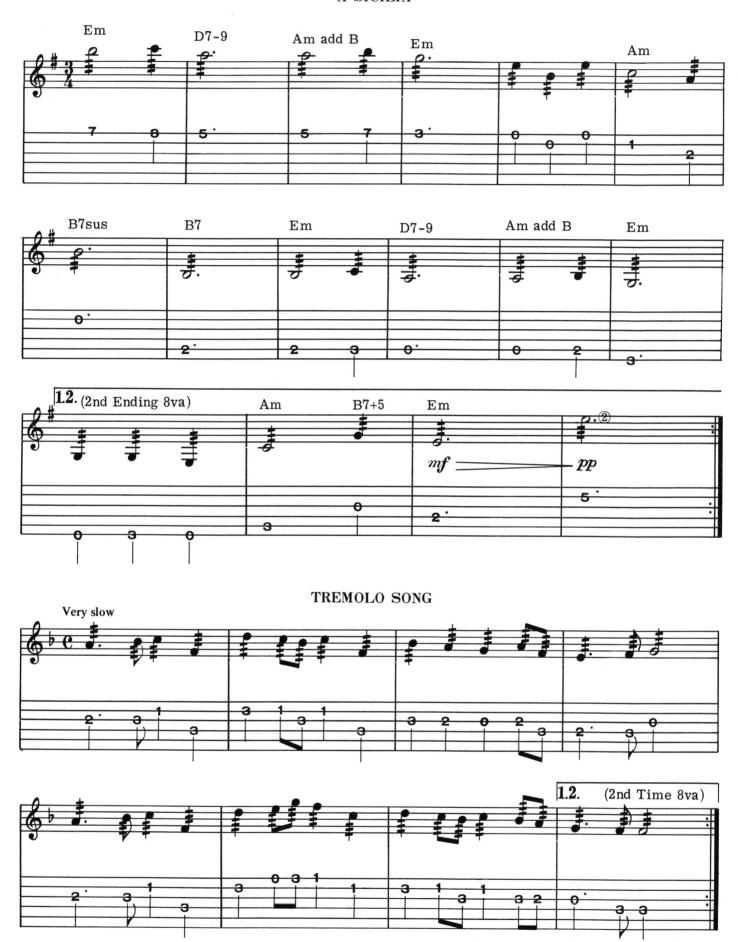

TREMOLO SONG

BALLADE

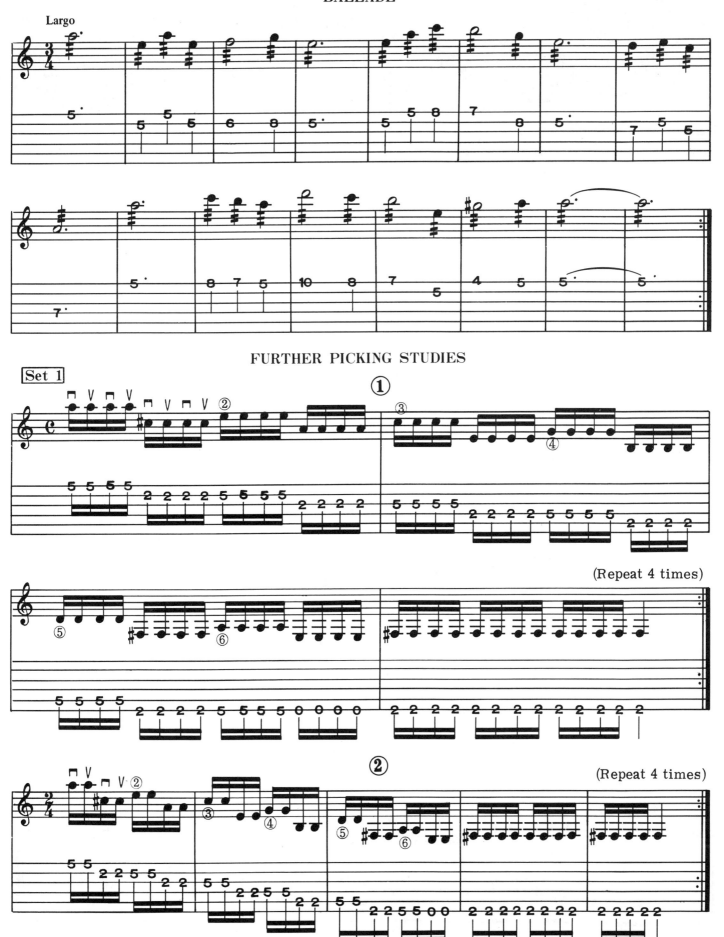

FURTHER PICKING STUDIES

Set 1

①

(Repeat 4 times)

②

(Repeat 4 times)

9

11

Set 2

12

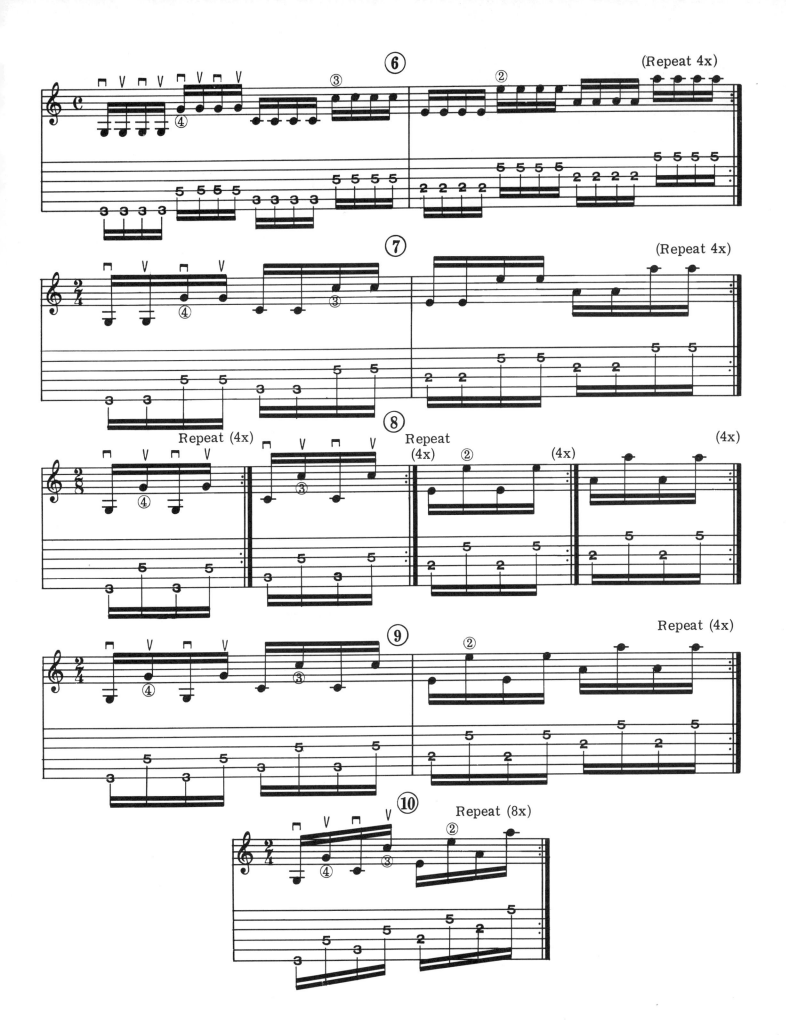

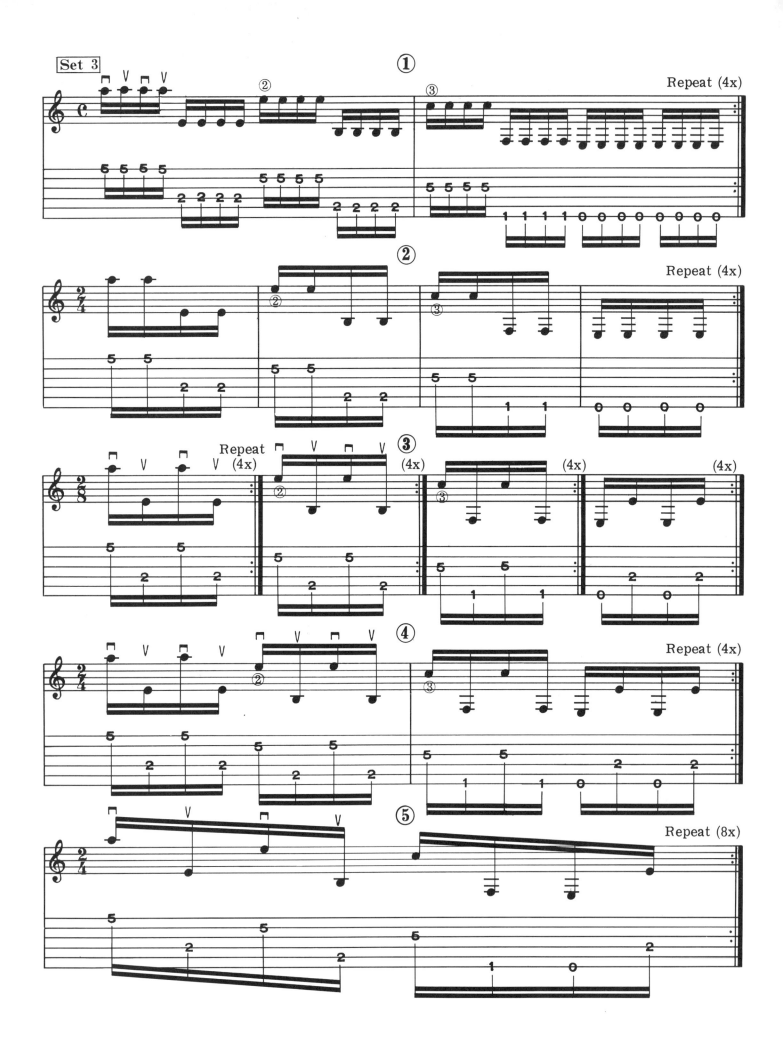

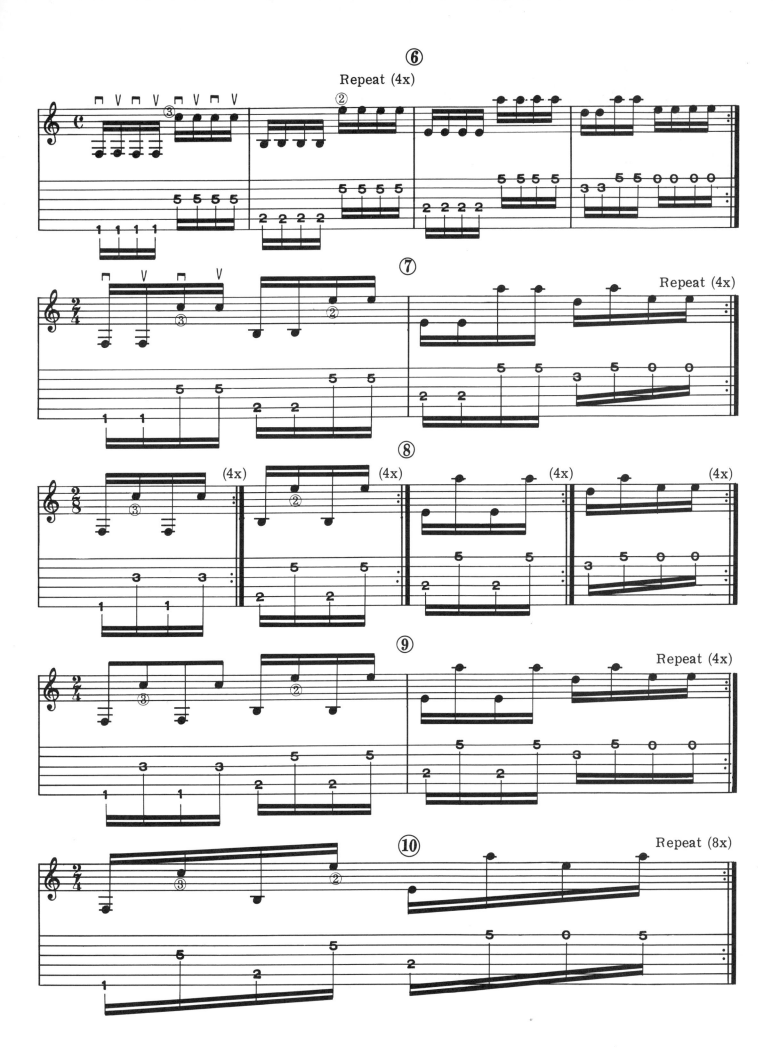

Set 4

PICKING ETUDE #1

PICKING ETUDE # 2

PICKING ETUDE #3

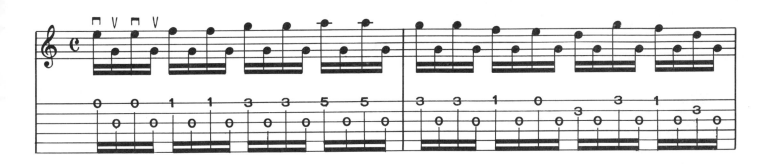

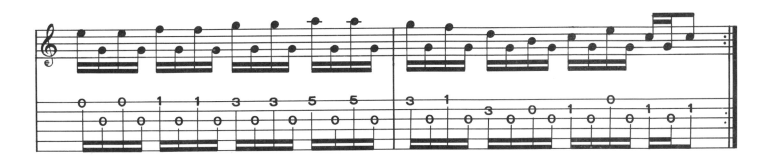

PICKING ETUDE #4

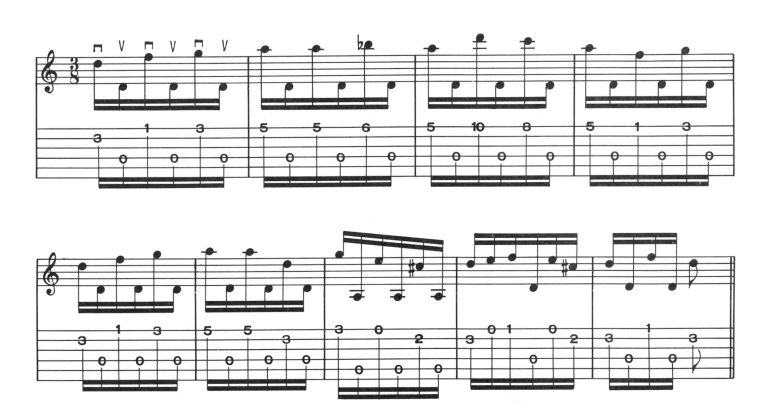

PICKING ETUDE # 5

PICKING ETUDE # 6

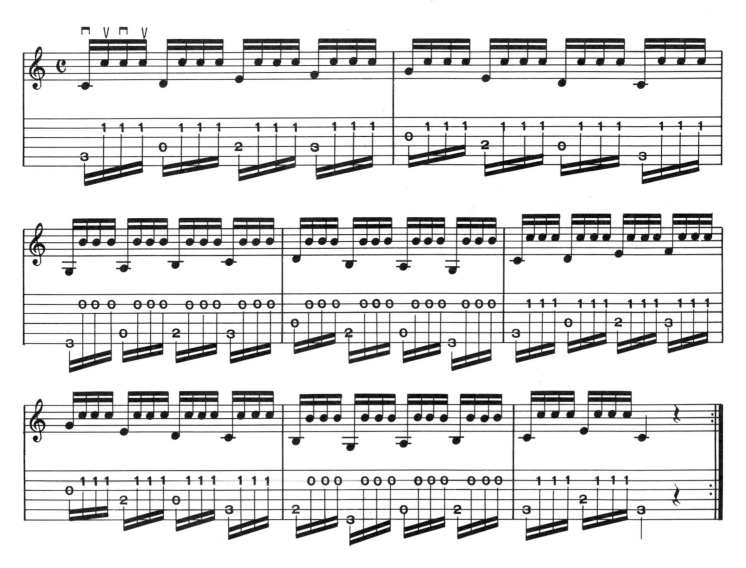

PICKING ETUDE # 7

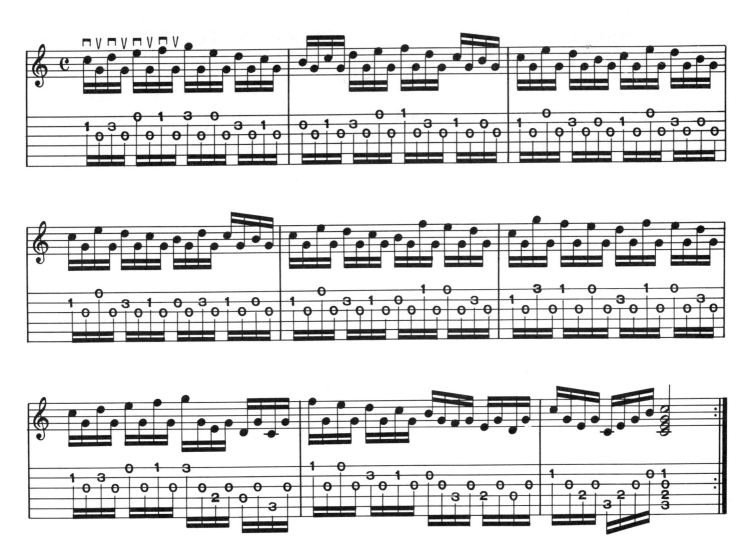

PICKING ETUDE # 8

PICKING ETUDE #9

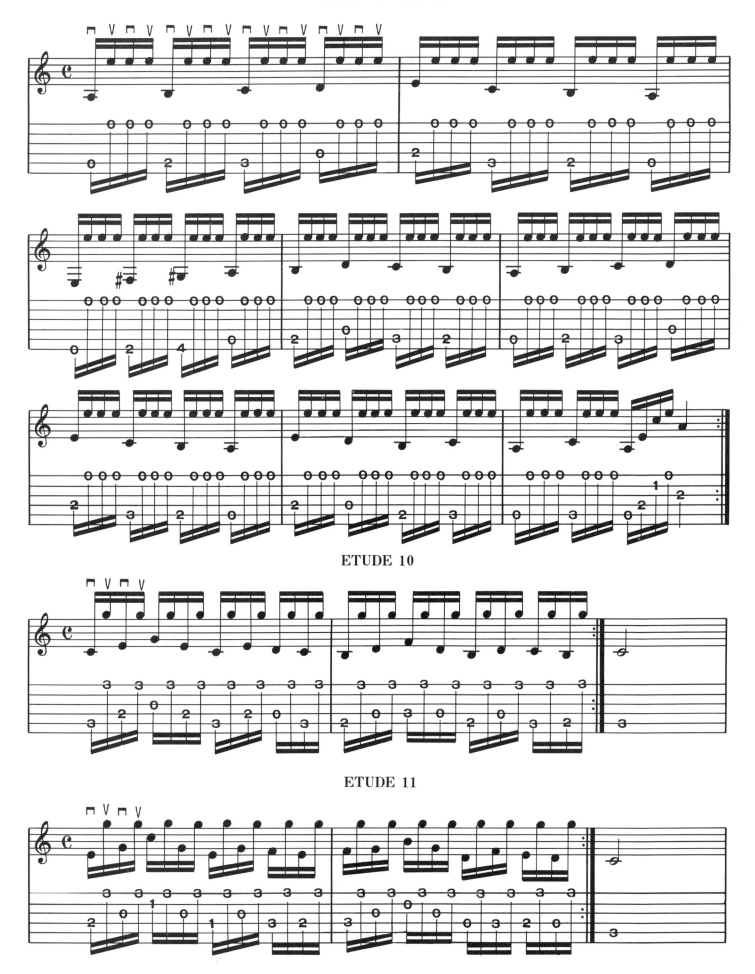

ETUDE 10

ETUDE 11

ETUDE 12

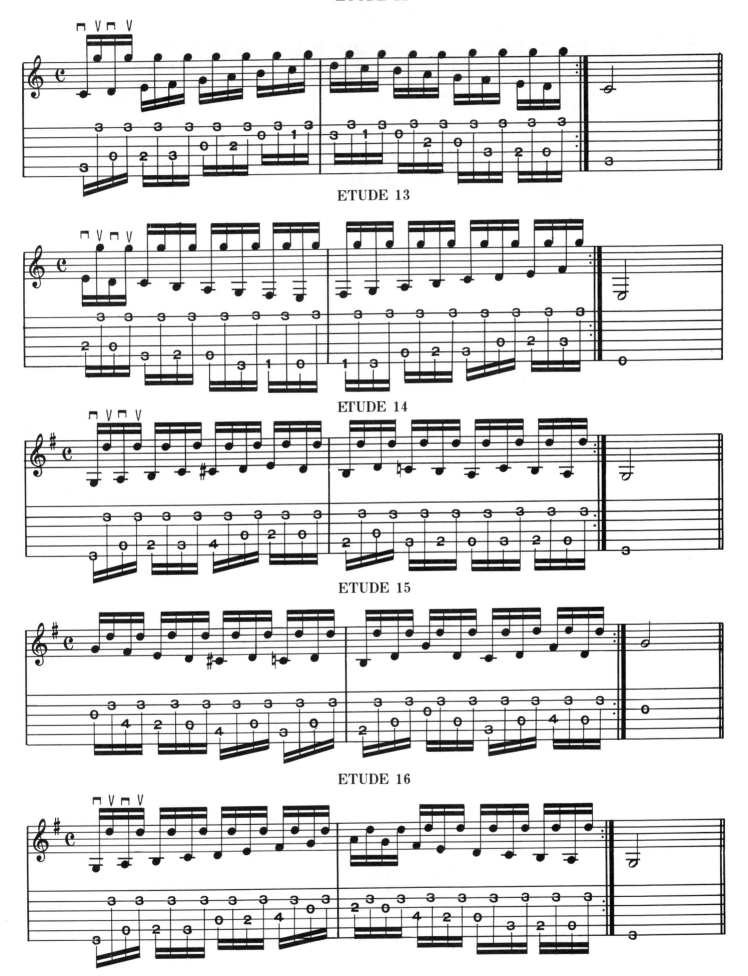

ETUDE 13

ETUDE 14

ETUDE 15

ETUDE 16

23

ETUDE 17

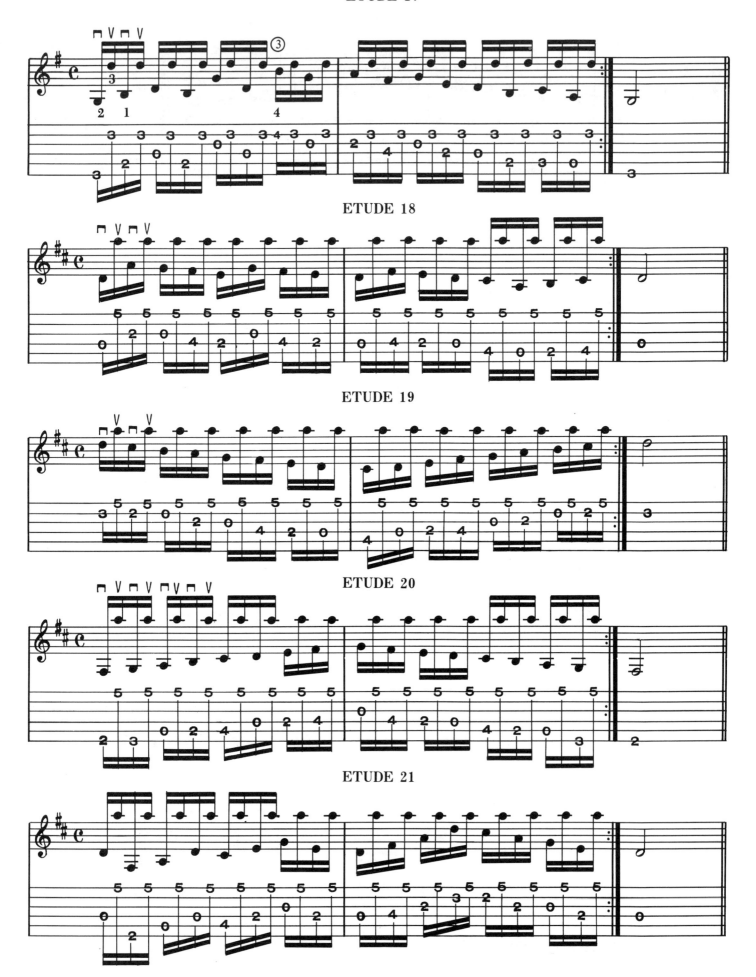

ETUDE 18

ETUDE 19

ETUDE 20

ETUDE 21

TRIPLET STUDIES
STUDY #1

STUDY #2

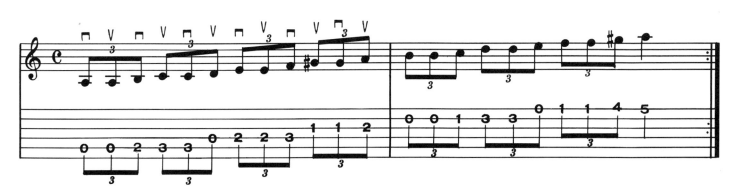

STUDY #3

Bill Bay

BARCELONA

Bill Bay

Mel Bay

TRIPLET STUDY #5

Aguado–Bay

JAZZ STUDY ♯ 1

Note: Student may also practice these studies with ⊓⊓⊓ ∨∨∨ picking. Make sure, however, notes should even in time valve.

Bill Bay

JAZZ STUDY ♯ 2

Practice: ⊓ ⊓ ⊓ ∨ ∨ ∨
and ⊓ ∨ ⊓ ∨ ⊓ ∨

Bill Bay

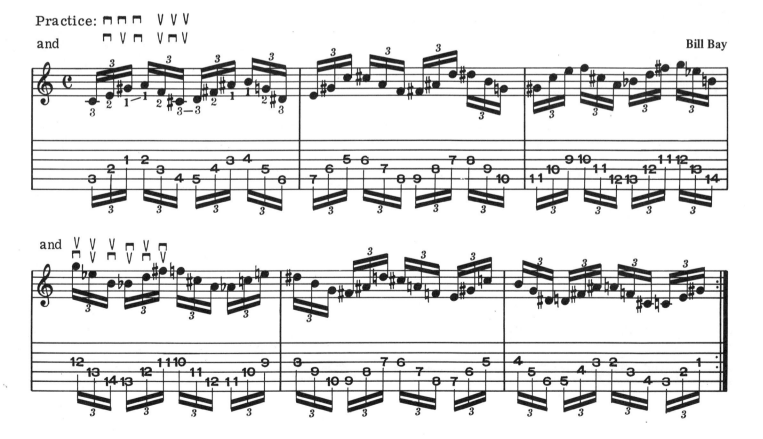

JAZZ STUDY ♯ 3

Use ⊓⊓⊓ ∨∨∨
and ⊓∨⊓ ∨⊓∨

Bill Bay

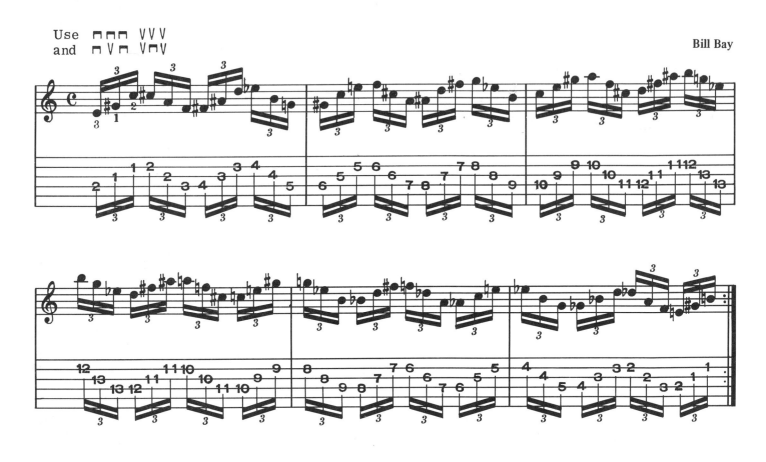

JAZZ STUDY ♯ 4

Use ⊓⊓⊓ ∨∨∨
and ⊓∨⊓ ∨⊓∨

Bill Bay

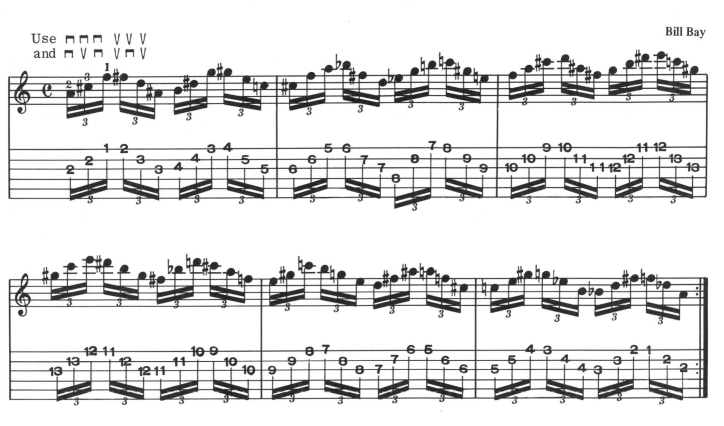

ADDITIONAL STUDIES

Practice: ⊓⊓⊓ＶＶＶ and ⊓Ｖ⊓ Ｖ⊓ Ｖ going up and coming down

Bill Bay

BILL'S ETUDE

Bill Bay

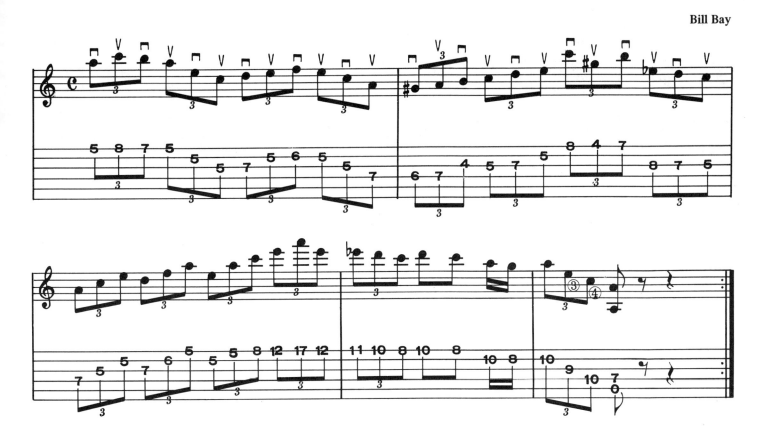

SOLILIQUY

Bill Bay

33

ANDANTE

Carcassi

SONG

Bill Bay

TRIPLET ETUDE #6

Carcassi

37

LESSON

Aguado

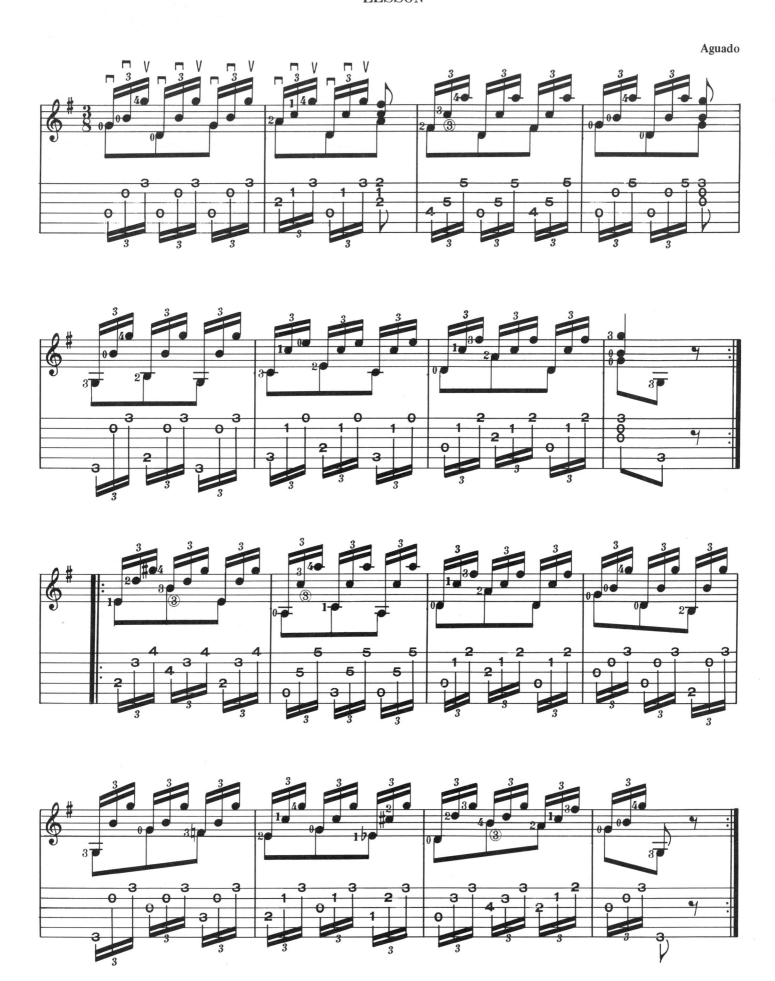

PRELUDE

Carcassi

Bill Bay

BLUES TRIPLET

MEDITATION

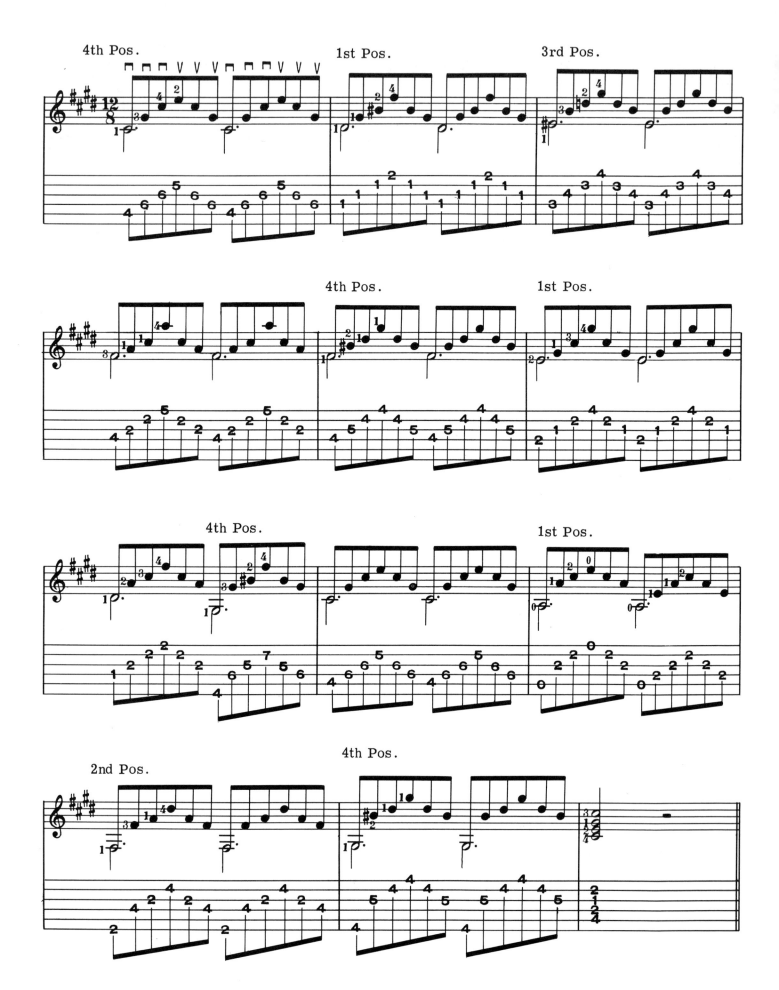

ANDANTE IN Bm

Bill Bay

ANDANTE

43

ALLEGRO BRILLANTE

Use Alternate Picking

Carcassi-Bay

45

ALLEGRO

Use Alternate Picking

6th Pos.

Carcassi-Bay

46

47

STUDY BY KREUTZER

Arr. B. Bay

Use Alternate Picking

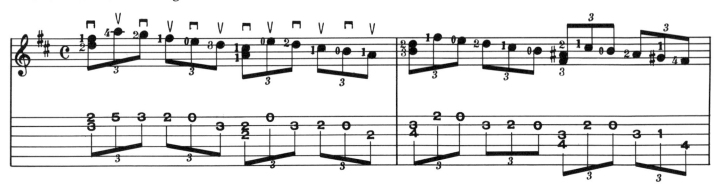

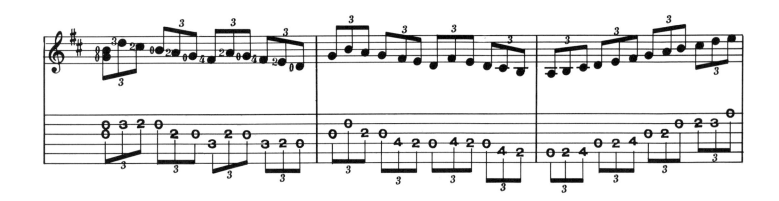

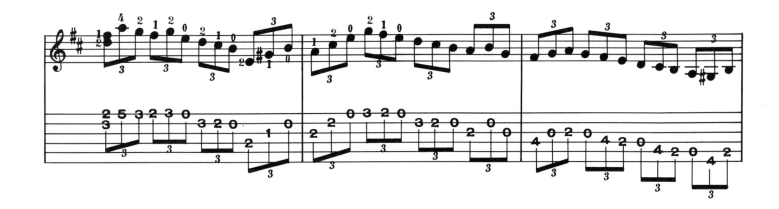

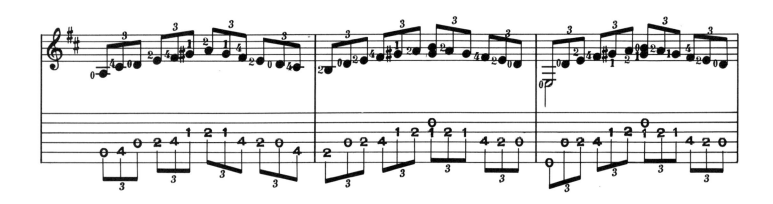

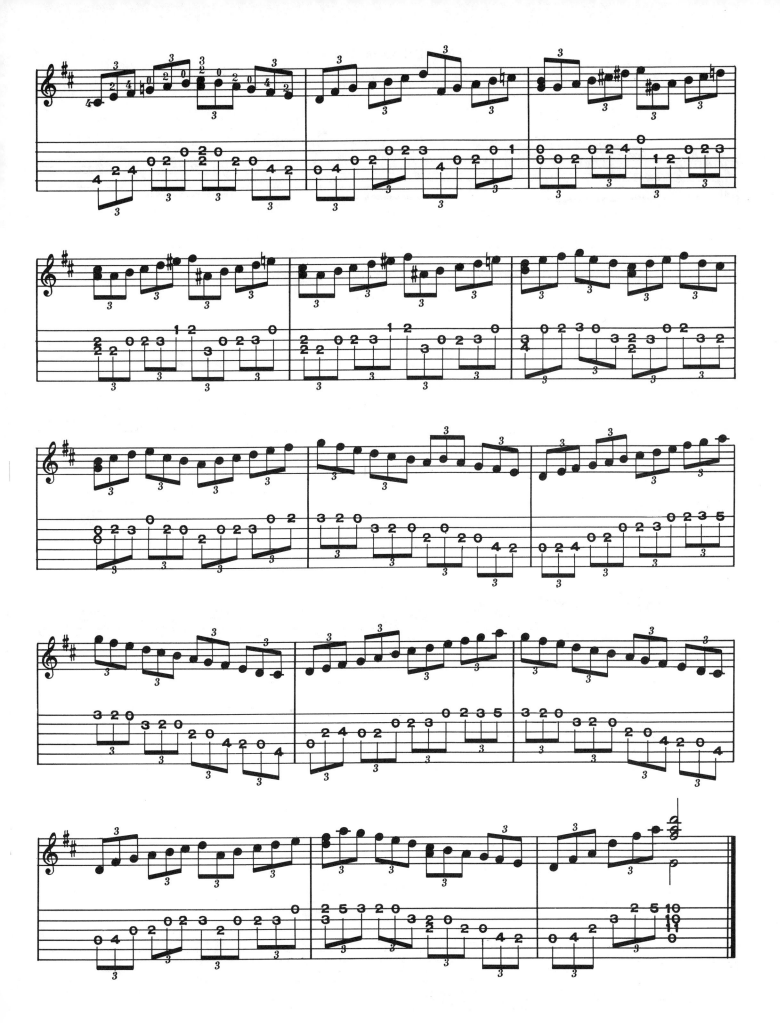

PRELUDE IN A MAJOR

Tarrega

ROMANZA – THEME

Composer Unknown

51

PRELUDIO

Diabelli

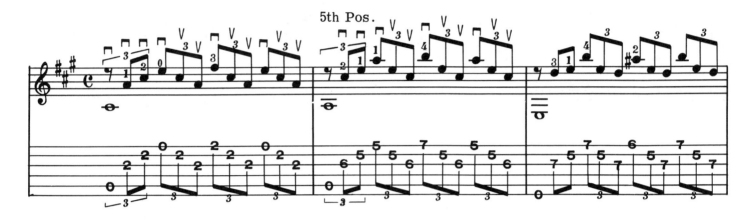

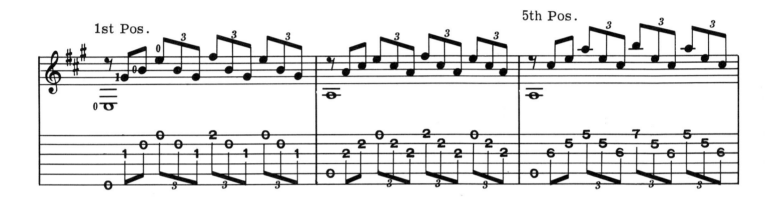

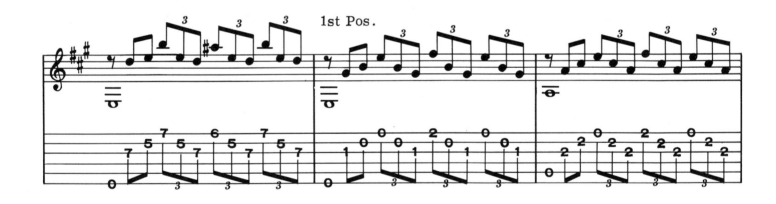

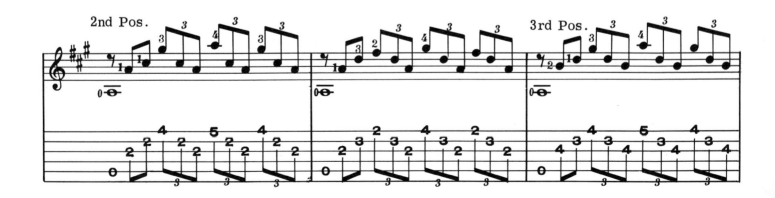

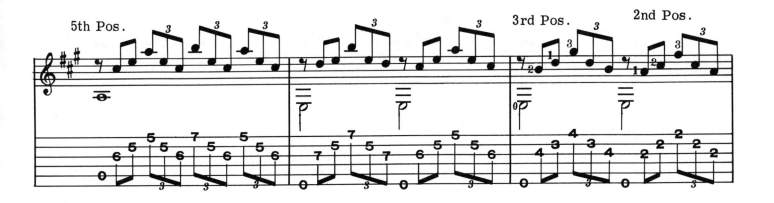

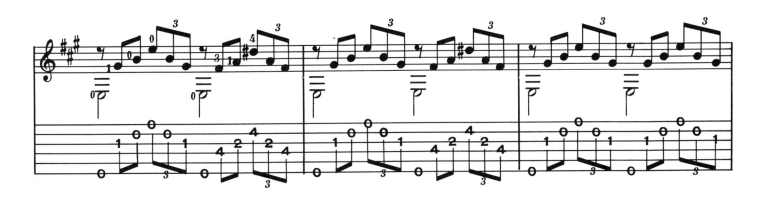

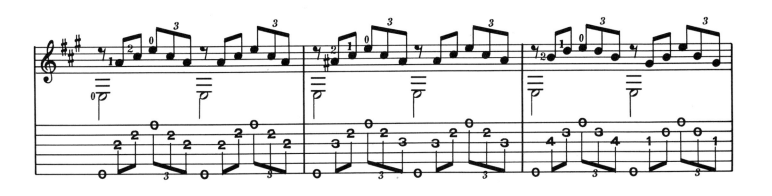

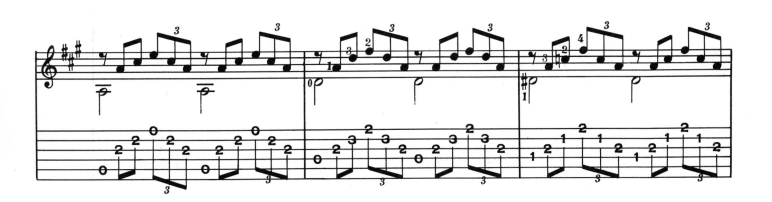

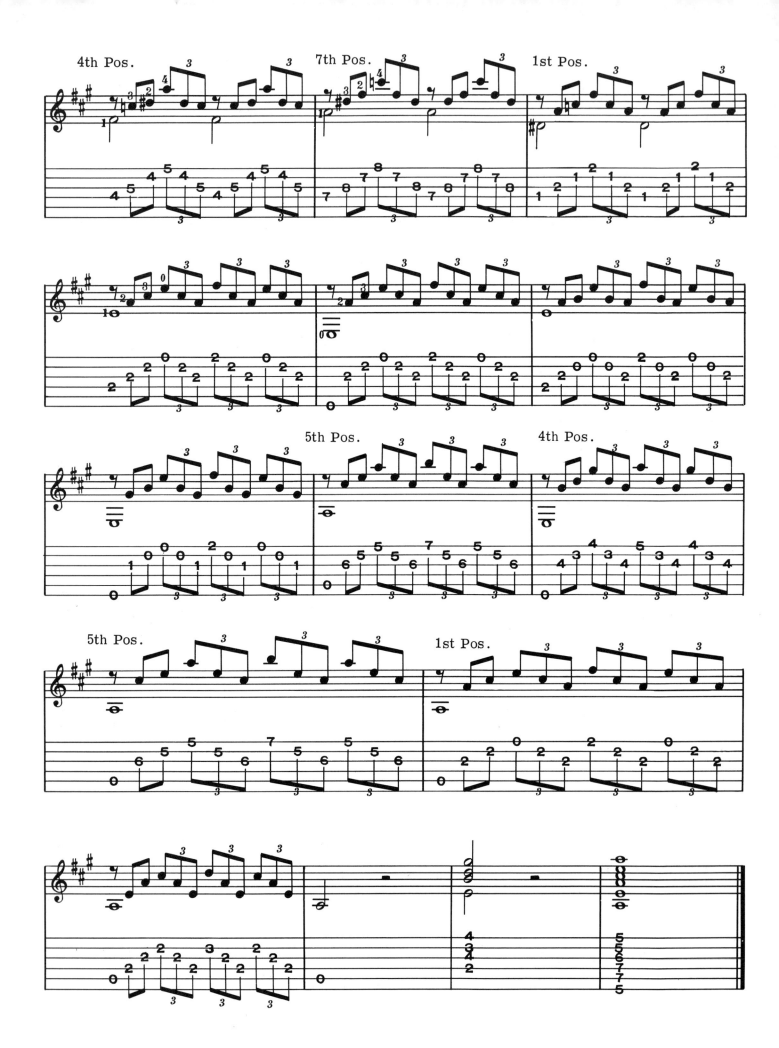

54

PRELUDIO

Coste

ARPEGGIO ETUDE

Aguado

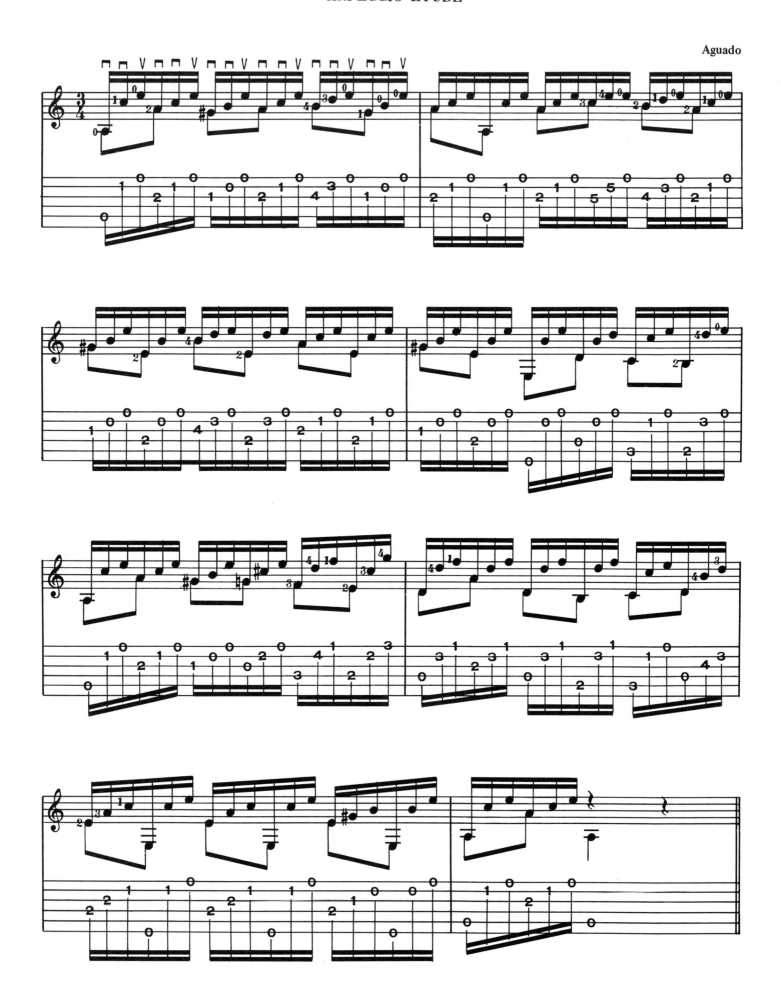

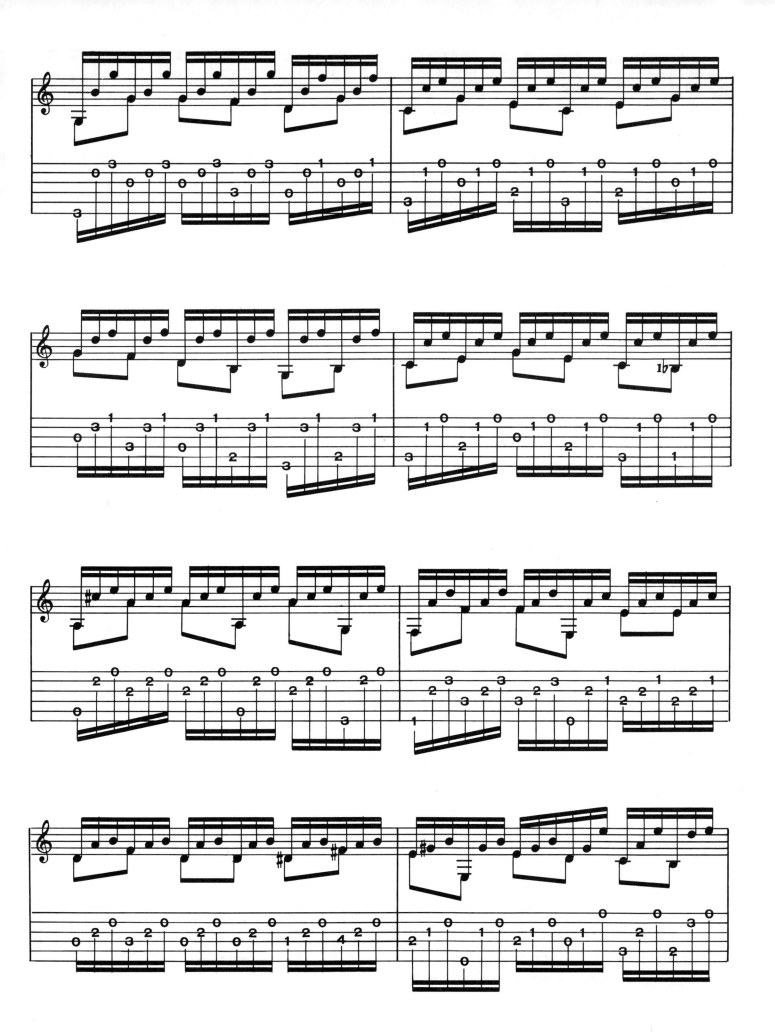

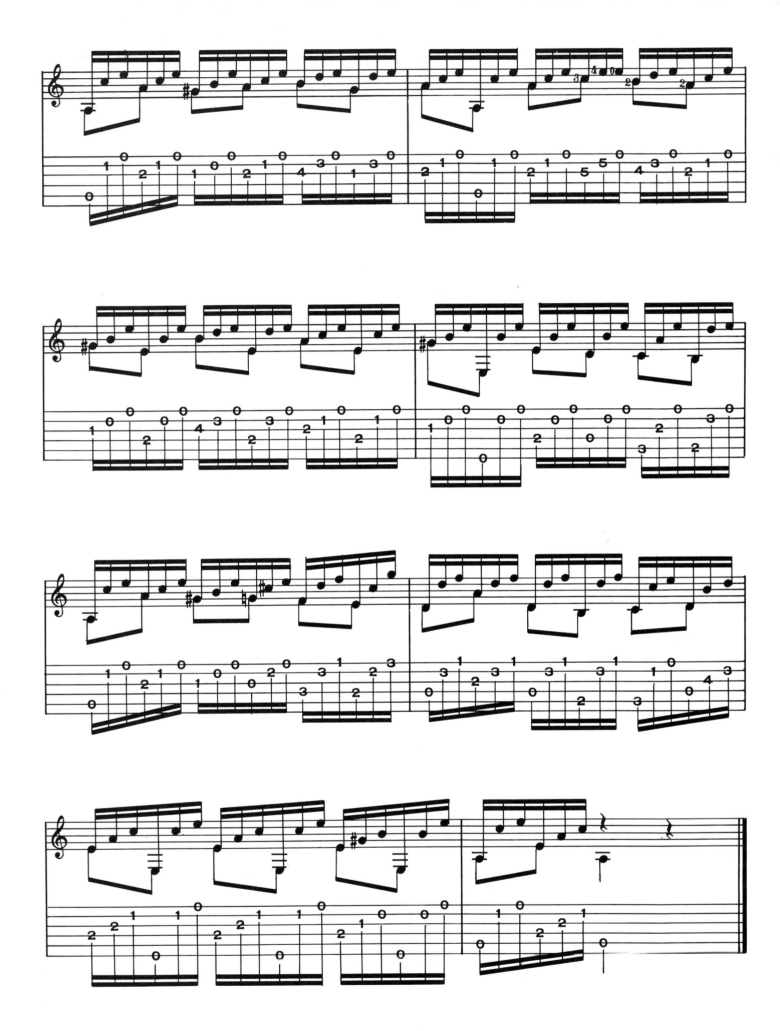

THE RAMBLING PITCHFORK

Irish Tune

59

TOBIN'S JIG

Irish Tune

60

11 MILE CANYON

Bill Bay

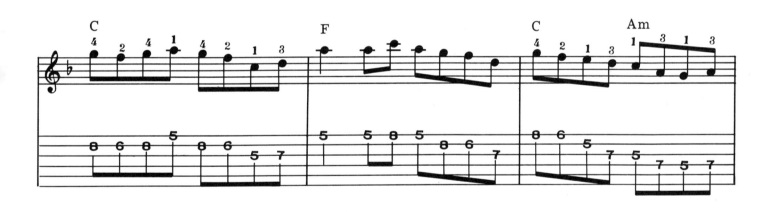

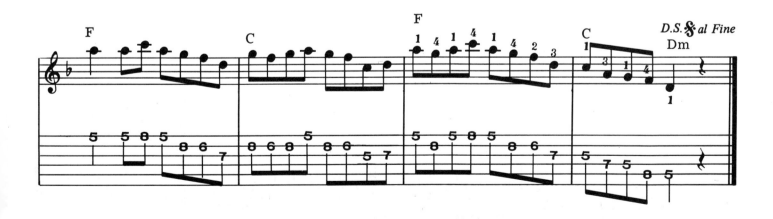

REAL REEL

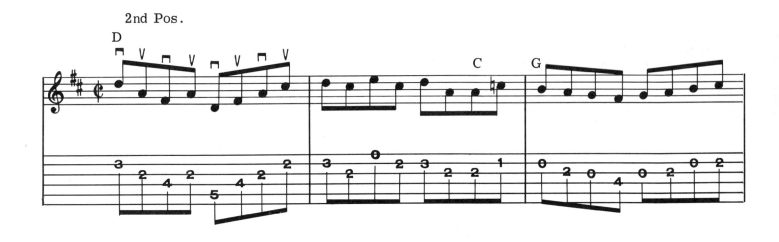

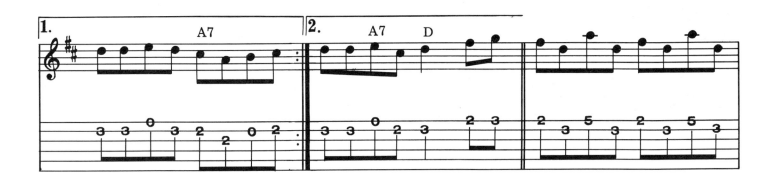

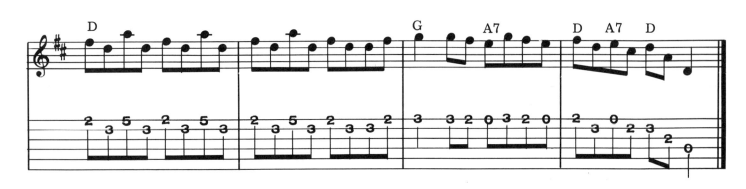

MODAL REEL

BOSTON BOY

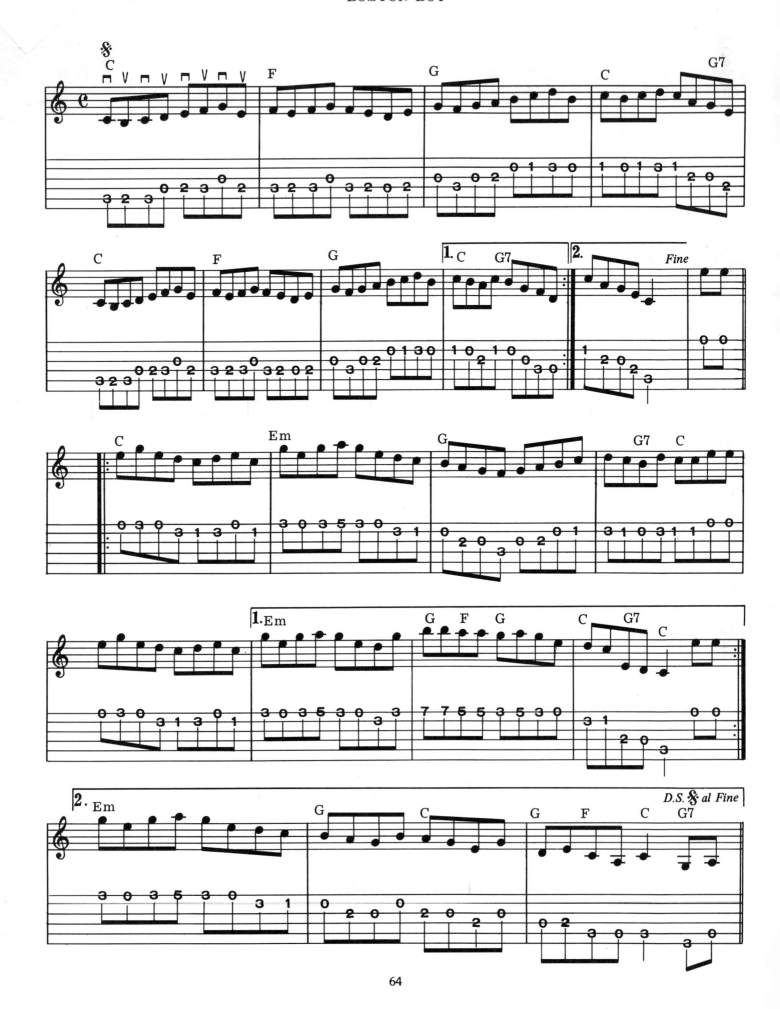

64

SOLDIER'S JOY

FISHER'S HORNPIPE

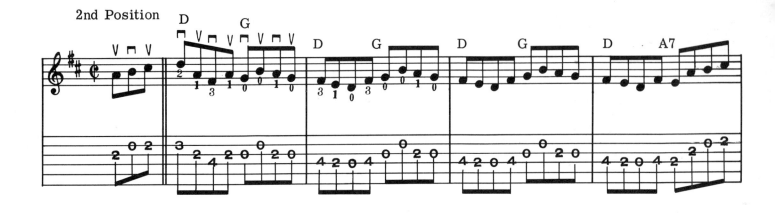

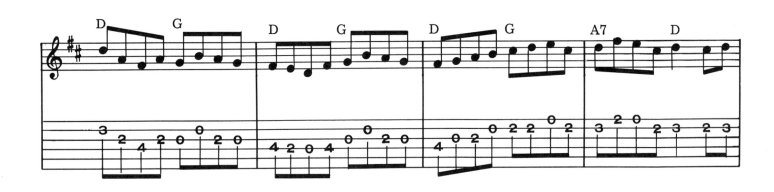

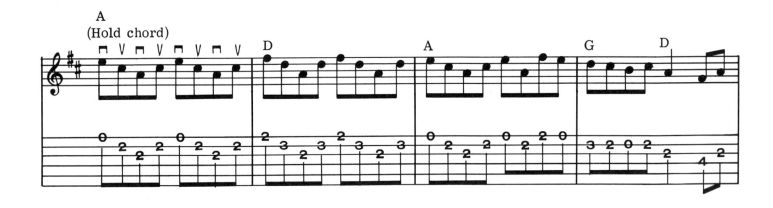

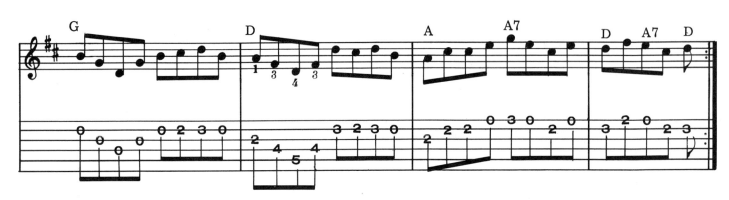

SAILOR'S HORNPIPE

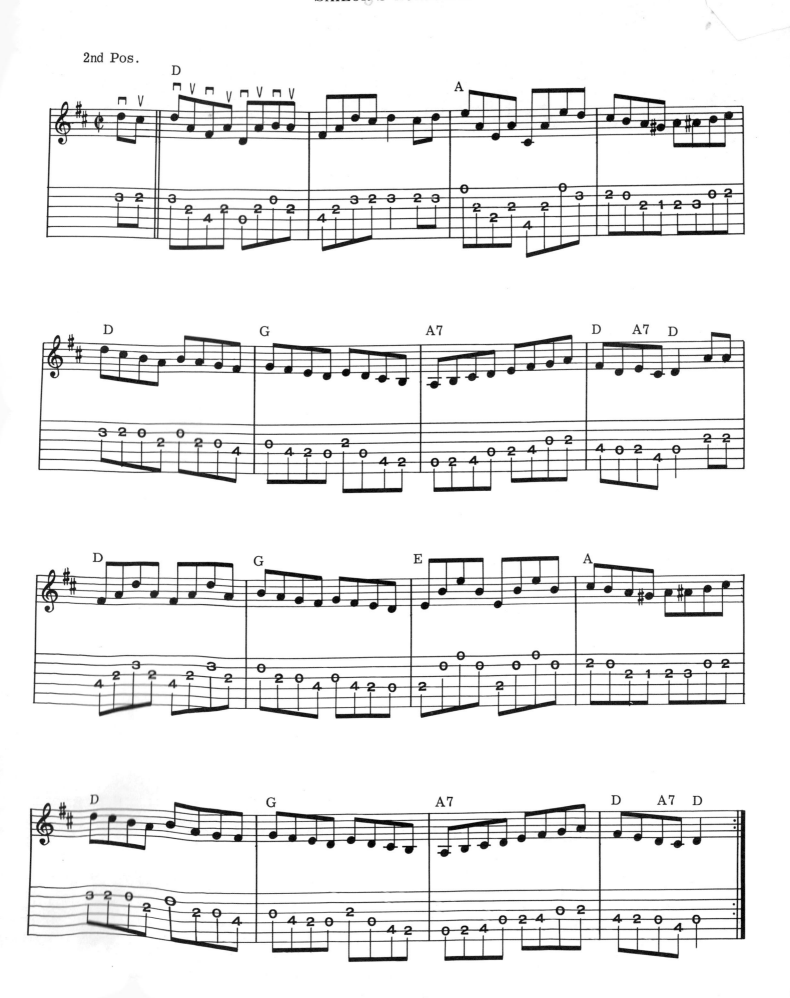

RAGTIME ANNIE

EIGHTH OF JANUARY

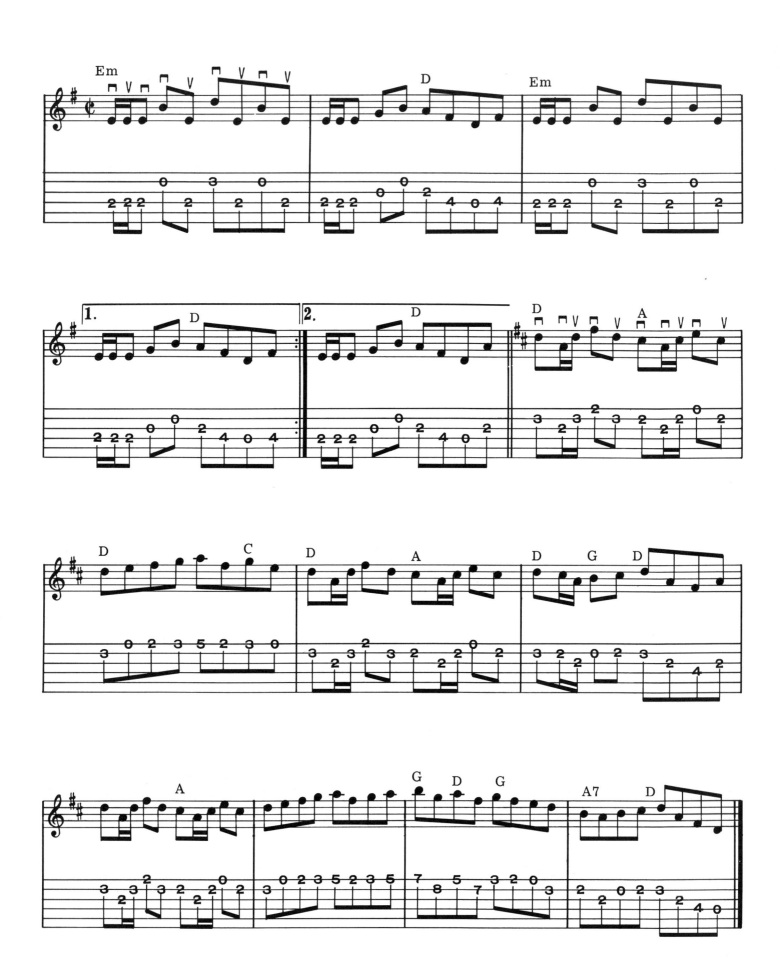

HARVEST HOME

PICKING ETUDE #1

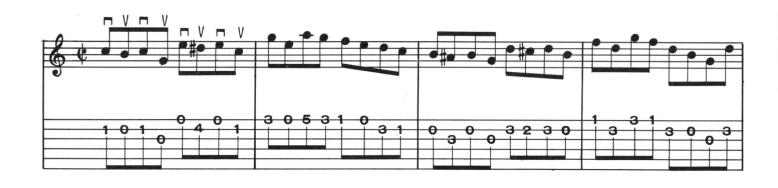

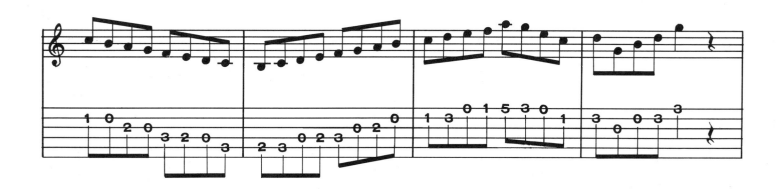

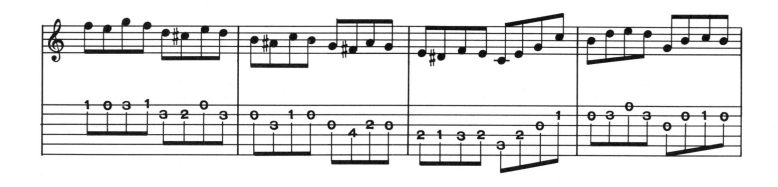

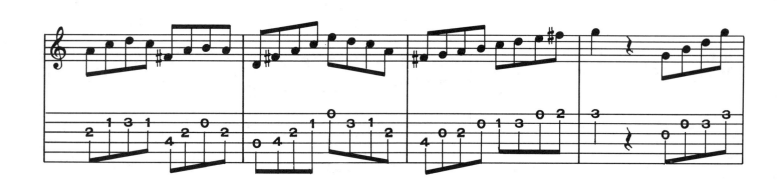

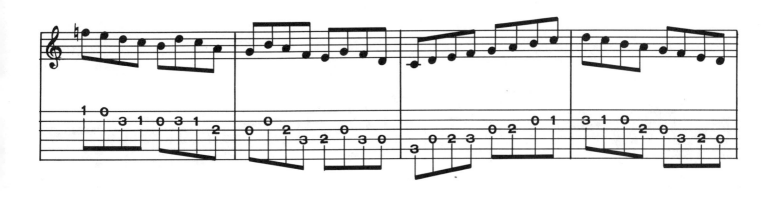

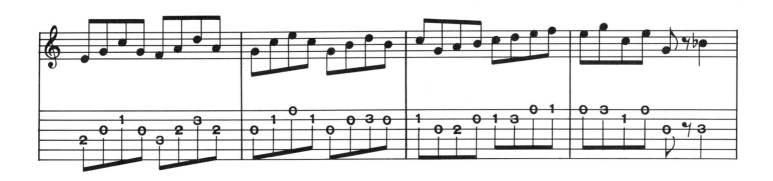

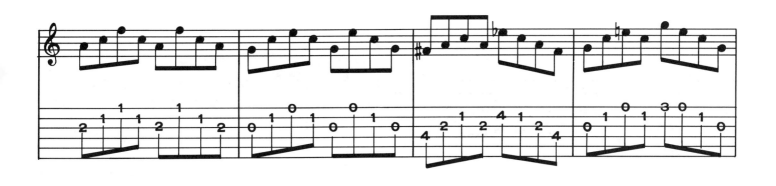

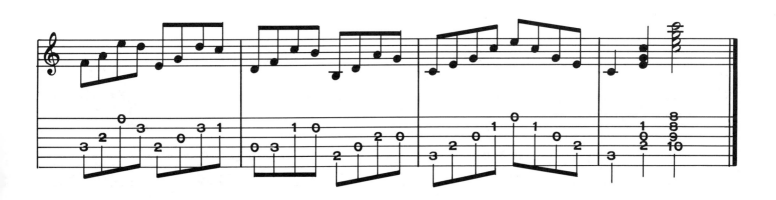

Carcassi

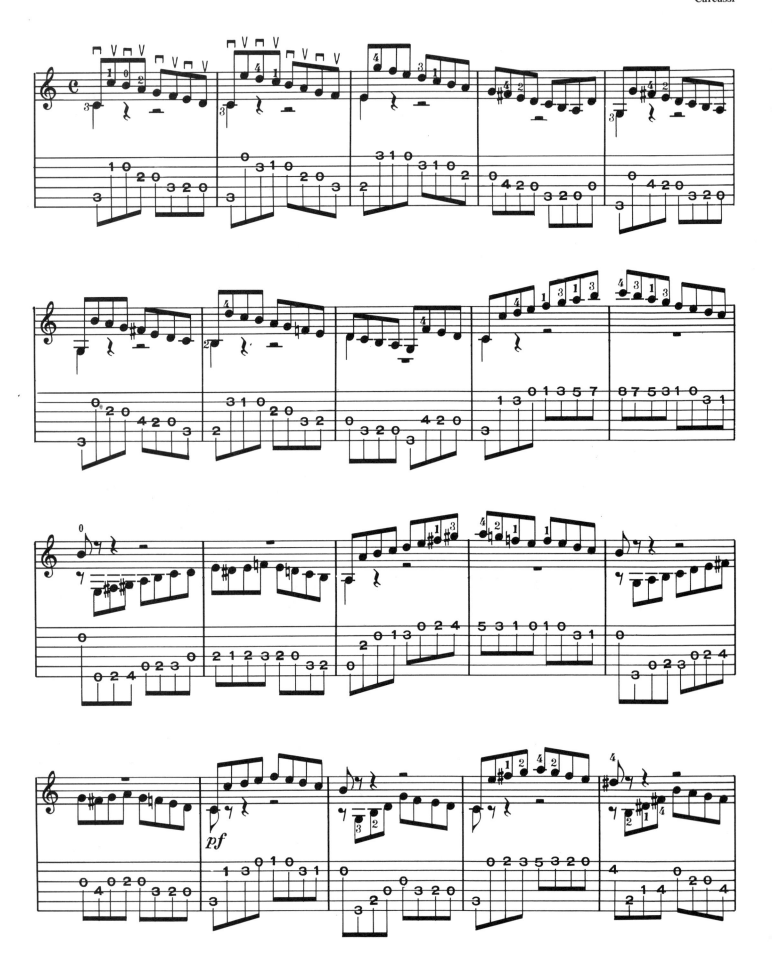

Carcassi-Bay

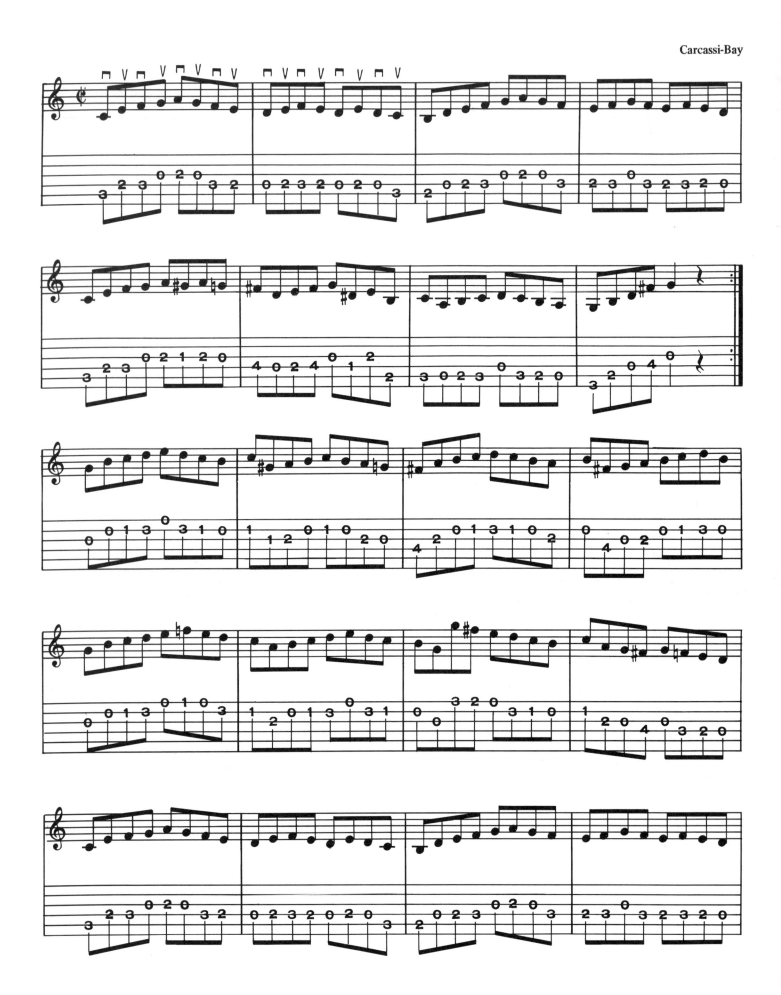

STUDY #14

Carcassi-Bay

78

ETUDE

Carulli

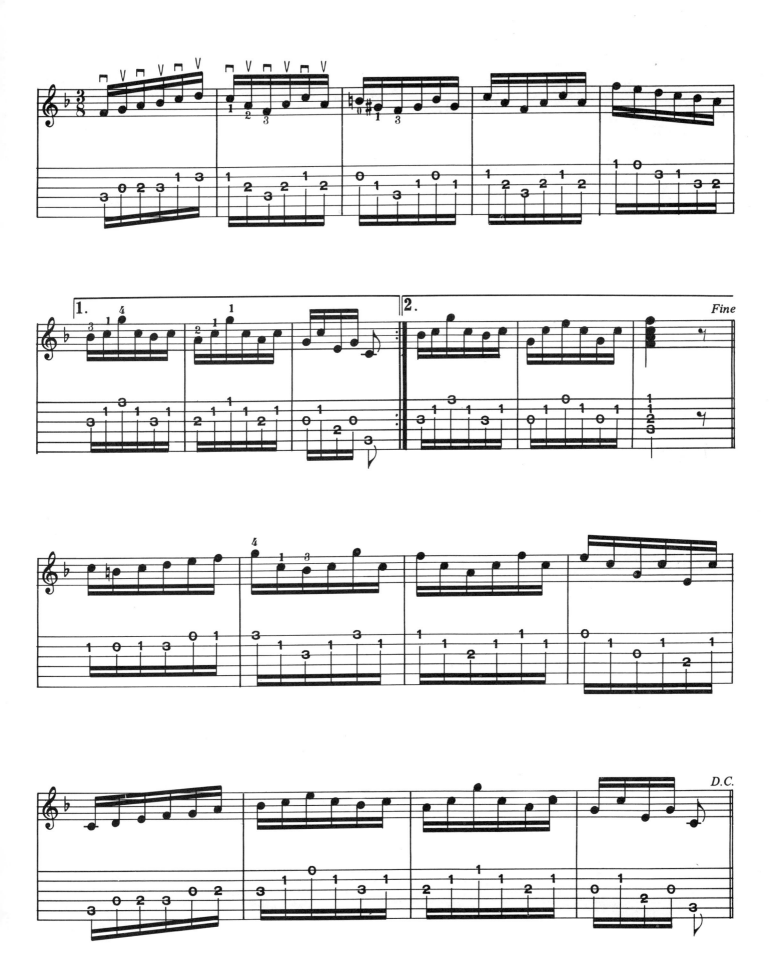

STUDY

Julian Arcas

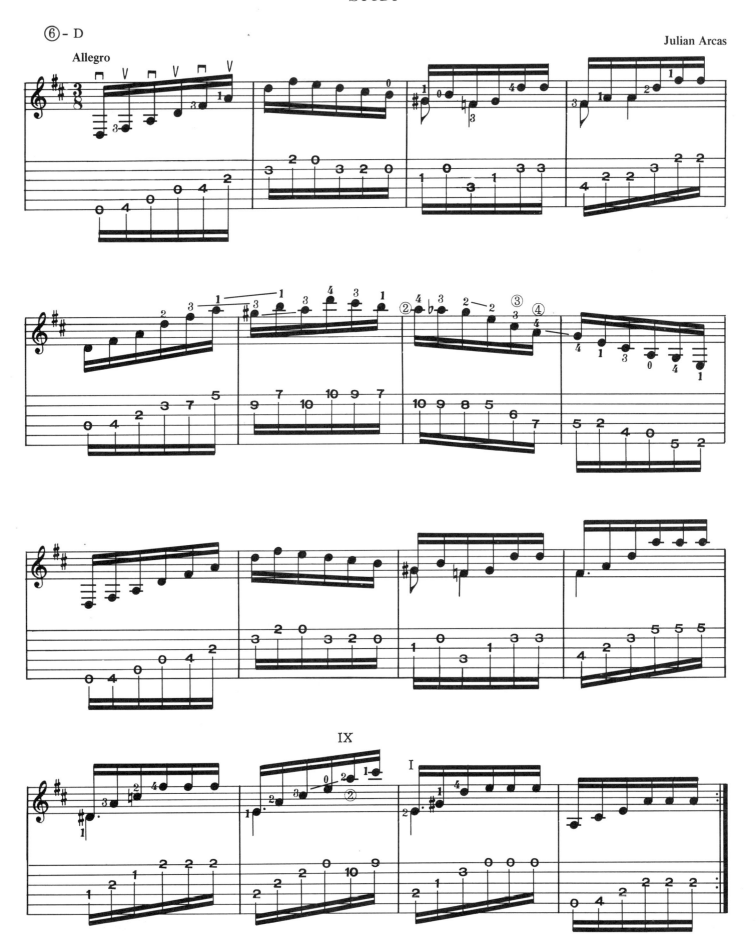

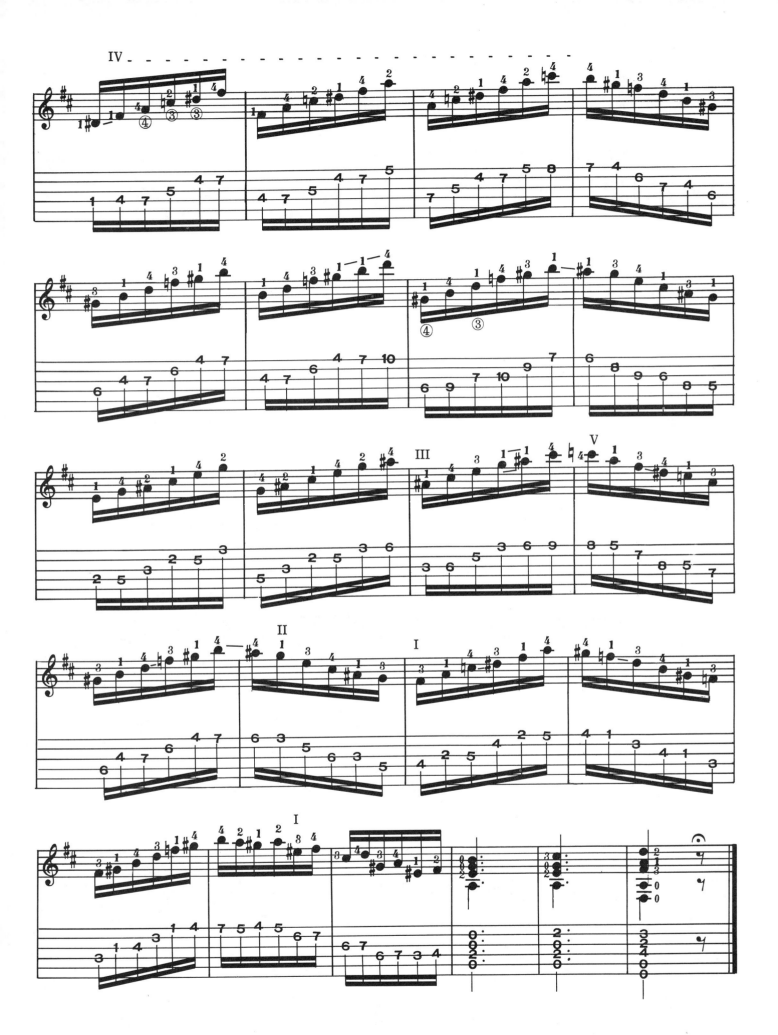

MUSIC TO PICK BY

Carulli

PRELUDE IN E MINOR

Giuliani

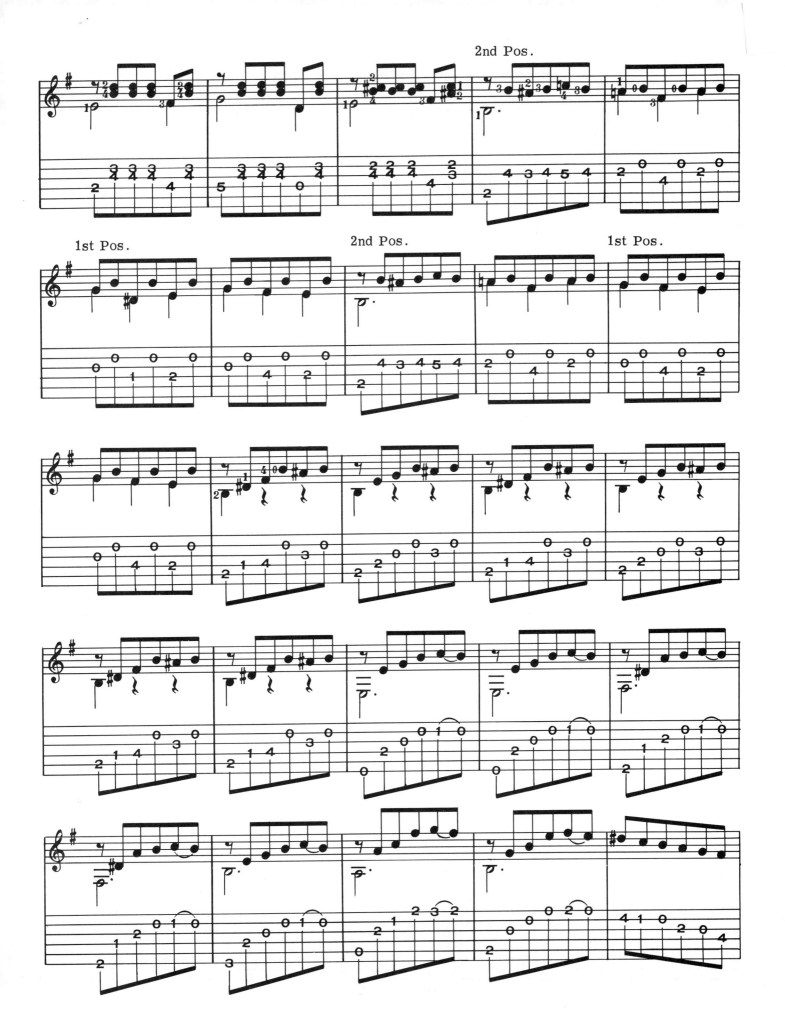

2nd Pos.

1st Pos.   2nd Pos.   1st Pos.

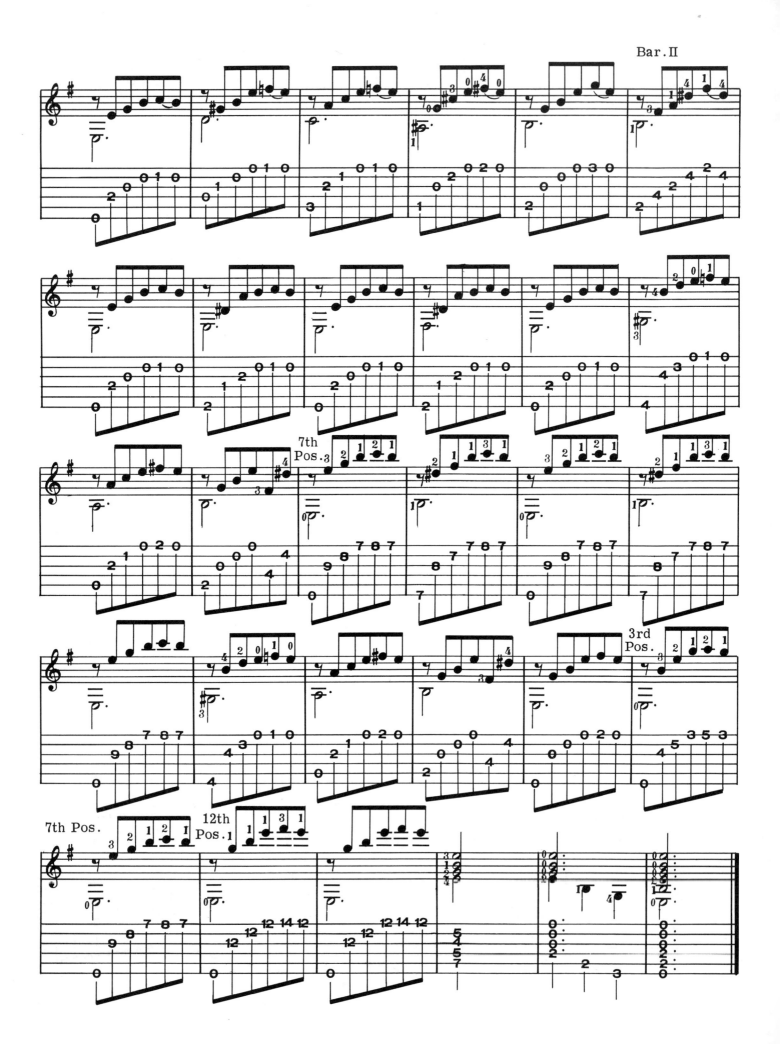

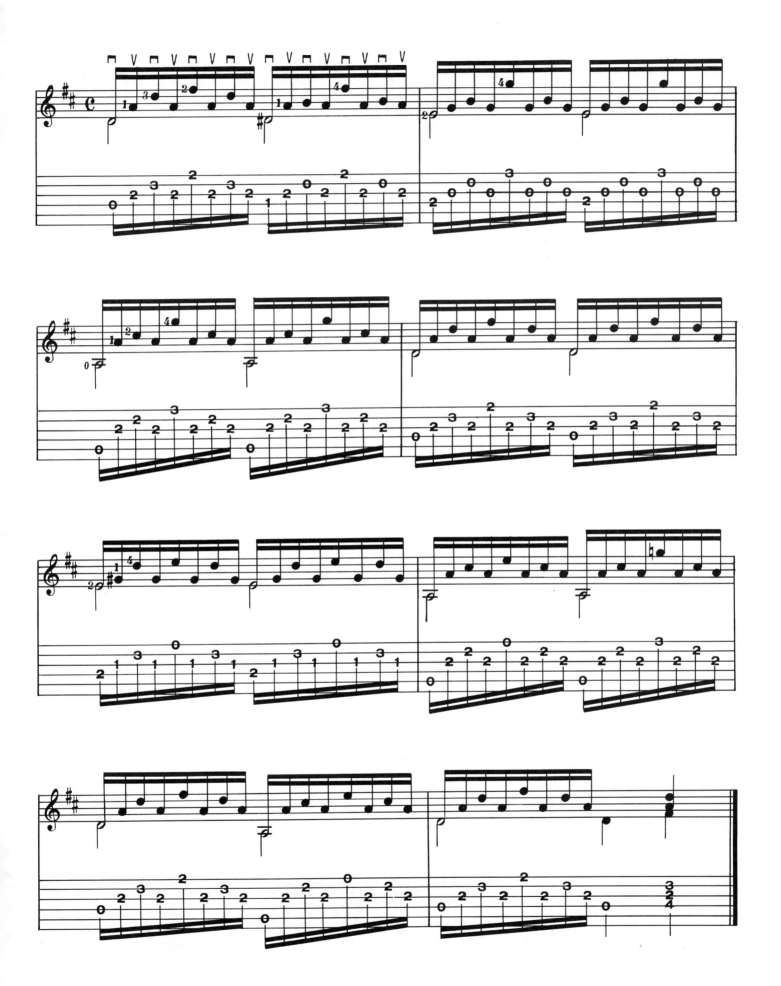

PRELUDE IN C MAJOR

J.S. Bach

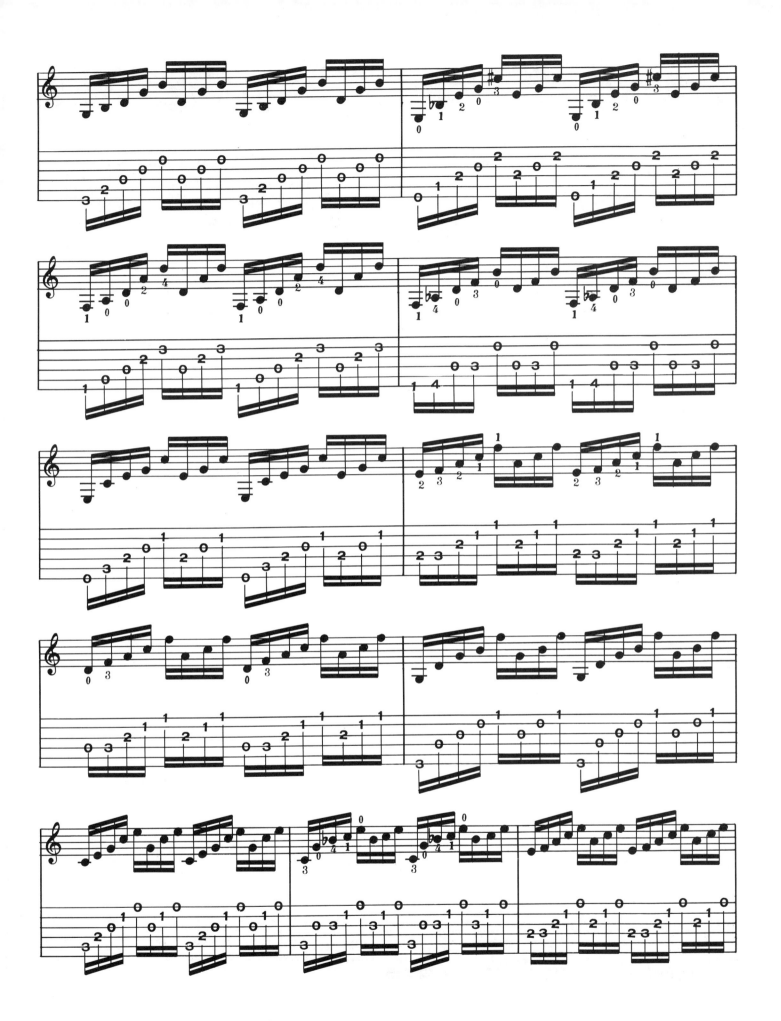

STUDY

Sor

93

CAPRICE IN D MINOR

Carcassi

PRELUDE IN A MAJOR

Sor

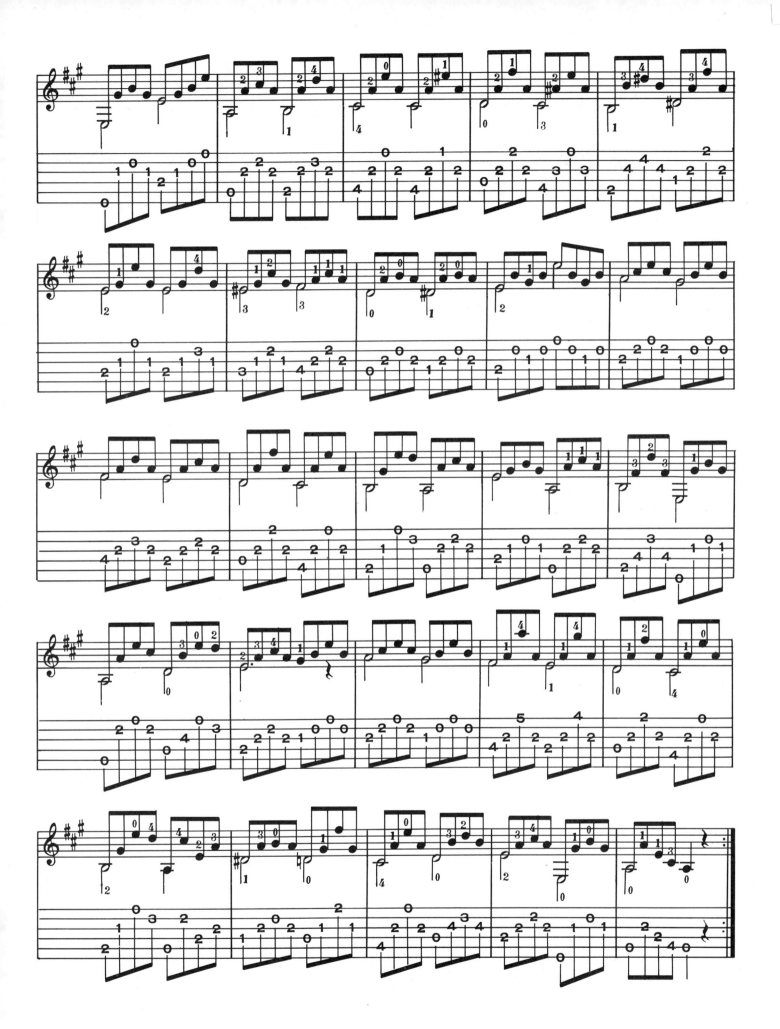

ETUDE

Mozzani

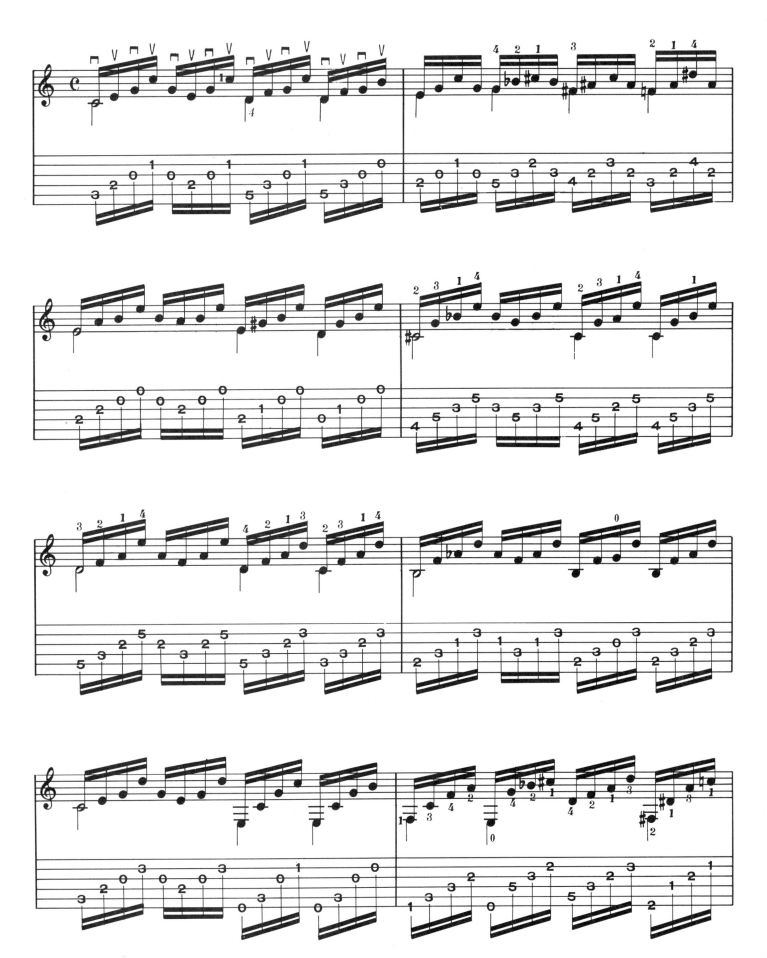

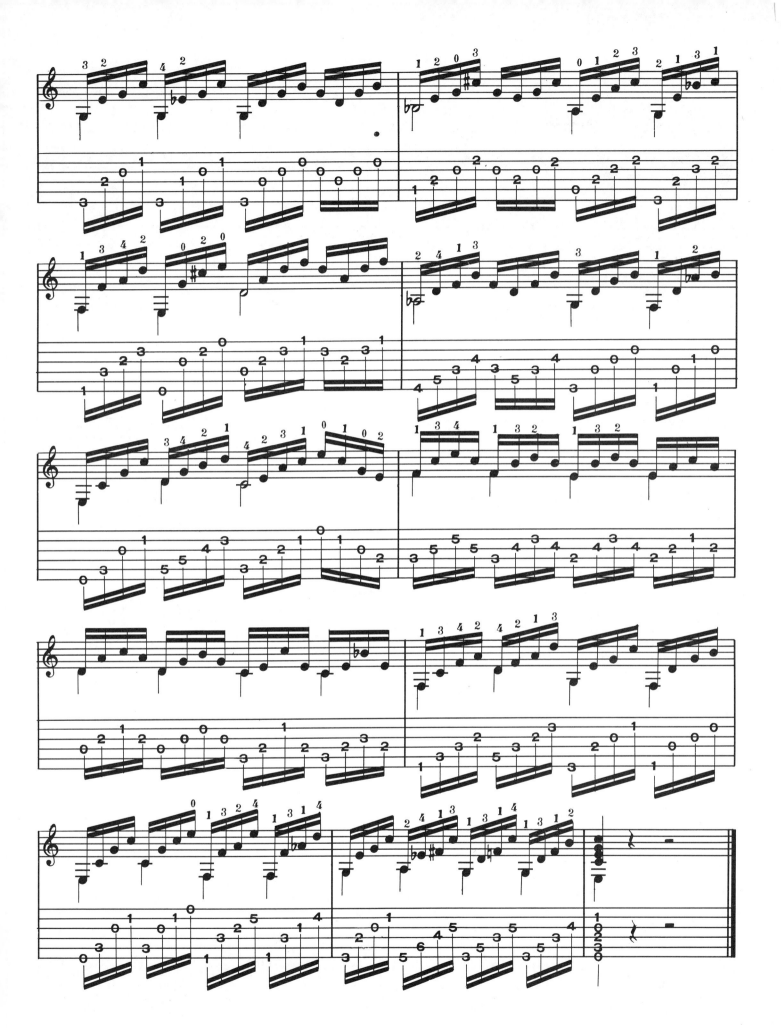

PRELUDE 1

Anton Diabelli

STUDY #1

Harry Volpe

scherzando

STUDY # 2

Carcassi

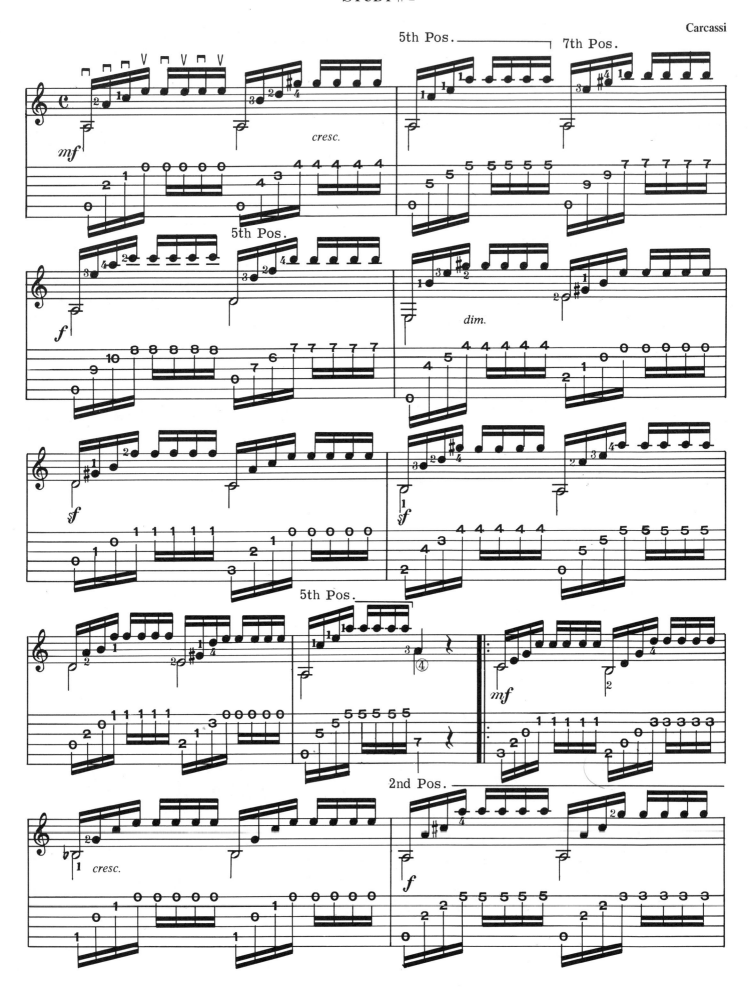

Carcassi

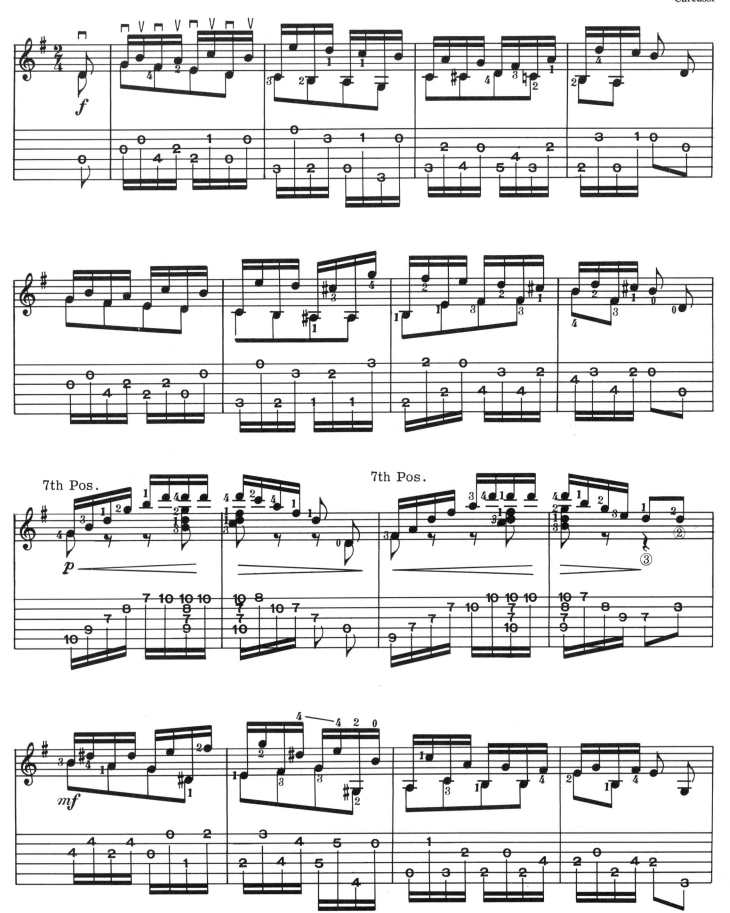

STUDY #7

Carcassi-Bay

110

3rd Pos.

PRELUDE NO. 5

Molino

113

LE PETITE MOULIN

Allegretto

Camille Saint Saëns

115

PRELUDE IN F MINOR

PRELUDE IN D♭

PRELUDE IN C MINOR

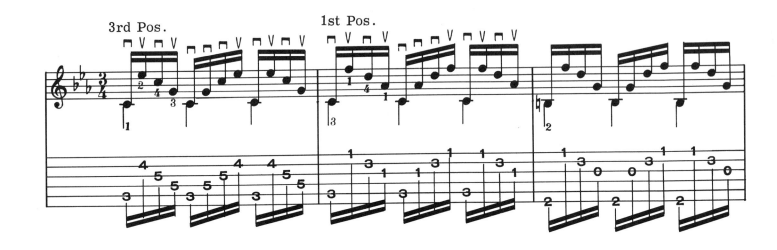

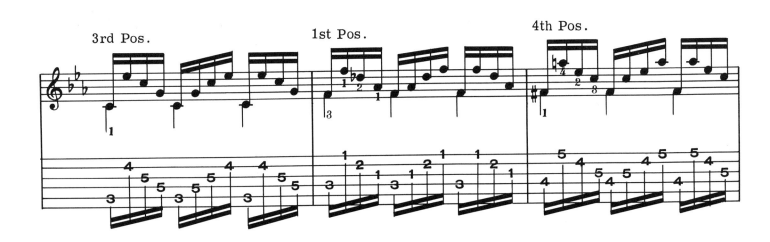

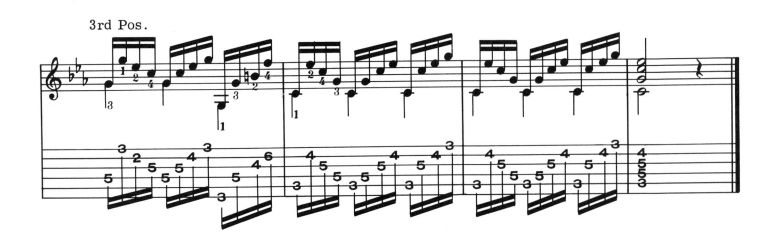

STUDY #8

Carcassi-Bay

PRELUDE IN B MINOR

Sor

Bar.II

Barre IV

Bar.II

121

CAPRICE

Giuliani

STUDY #15

Carcassi-Bay

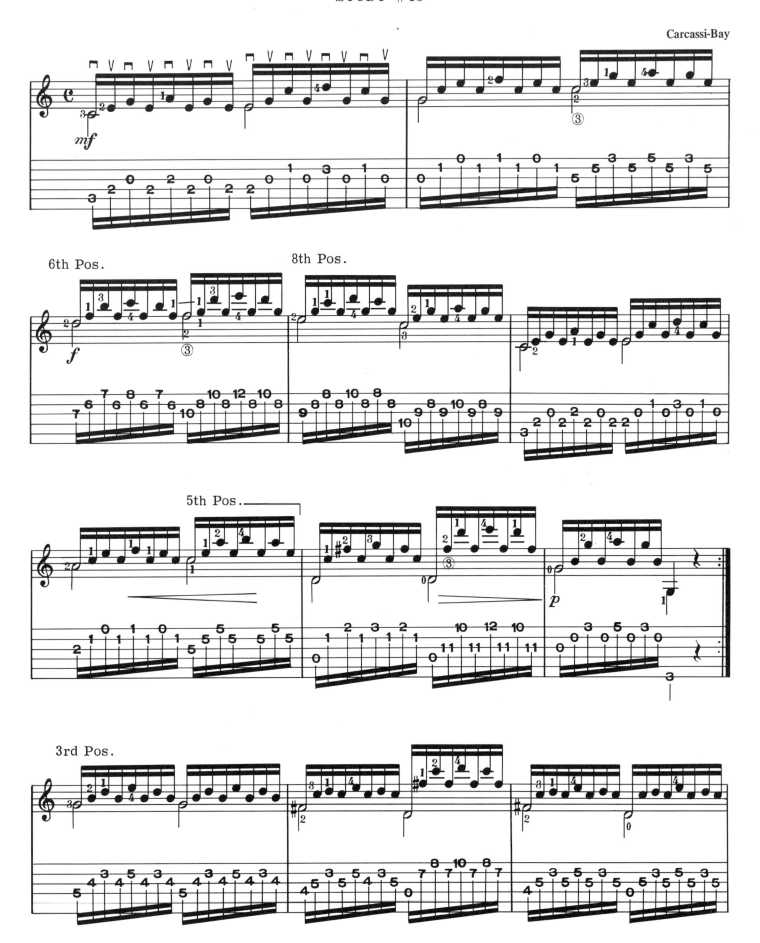

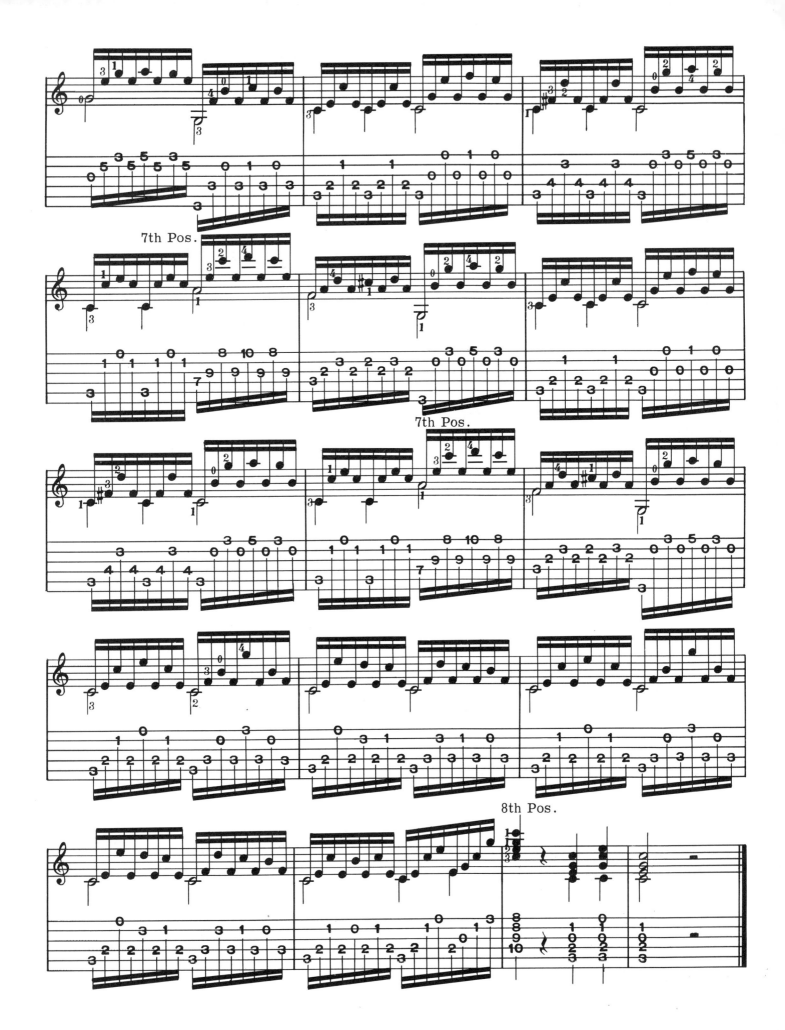

ETUDE IN G MINOR

STUDY #22

Carcassi-Bay

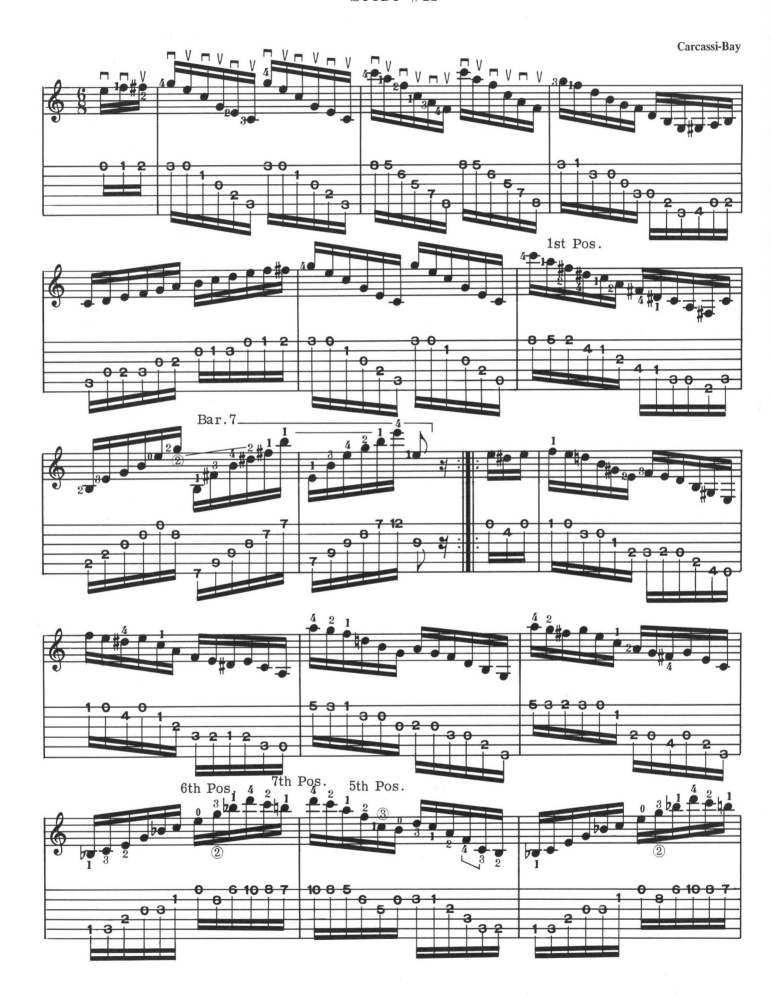

STUDY IN D MINOR

(Pick near the bridge for Harpsichord like effect)

Tarrega

OTHER MEL BAY BOOKS FOR THE SERIOUS GUITARIST

The Tom Bruner Series:
   Developing Melodic Sight Reading Technique
   How To Play Guitar In A Big Band
   Becoming a Professional Guitarist
   Playing Guitar For Motion Picture Soundtracks

Building Left Hand Technique
The Complete Johnny Smith Approach To Guitar
George Van Eps Harmonic Mechanisms Volume One
George Van Eps Harmonic Mechanisms Volume Two
George Van Eps Harmonic Mechanisms Volume Three
Guitar Fingerboard Harmony
Ivor Mairants' The Complete Guitar Experience
Deluxe Guitar Scale Book
Deluxe Guitar Arpeggio Studies
Guitar Improvising Volume One
Guitar Improvising Volume Two
Jazz Guitar Lines
Jazz Guitar Scales
Rhythm Guitar Chord Studies
Deluxe Guitar Chord Progressions
Art Of Solo Jazz Guitar
Fingerstyle Jazz Etudes
Complete Method For Modern Guitar

Great Music at Your Fingertips